DANCING WITH REDEMPTION

BARRE TO BAR
BOOK FIVE

SUMMER COOPER

LOVY BOOKS

1

Roxie

"You know, last night I told Lincoln I didn't know where you were. And that I'd tell him if I found out." Nick's voice broke into Roxie's thoughts, and she turned to see that boyish smile of his in place. He was enjoying making Lincoln squirm, that was obvious.

Roxie turned back to stare out of the window of his penthouse apartment, her voice smothered by the weight of her emotions, her eyes narrowed against the glare of morning sunshine. She could only nod in response, her arms wrapped tightly around her waist as if to hold everything inside that threatened to pour out if she opened her mouth.

She'd come to him after a lot of internal debate in

her car. Her thoughts had been too scattered to make any decision other than the one that had brought her here. Getting out of South Carolina and ending all of this drama about her past, once and for all, was the only answer. Lincoln would keep Lily safe, just as he'd keep her safe, if she allowed him that option.

Safety wasn't what she needed right now, answers were what she needed, and she wouldn't get those down here. A trip to New York, back to her old stomping grounds, might make them all safe again, if she could find out who'd killed her parents and put an end to a decade of hiding like a mouse.

The only problem was, Lincoln would find her if she went the commercial route. Nick had his own private jet, which meant he could get her out without Lincoln being any the wiser. That was exactly what Roxie wanted, anonymity and the peace to do what she needed to do.

"It figures he'd do that. I haven't even been gone that long." Roxie sat down on the black leather sofa in the living room, her eyes now on the man that would readily take Lincoln's place in her heart, if she'd let him. That wasn't an option either. Not because she didn't like Nick, but because Lincoln was irreplaceable, even if he was a giant dick sometimes. "I wonder if his little band of security people are staked out downstairs, waiting to see if I pop up."

"Hm, that is a concern. I'll arrange for a car with tinted windows, then they won't be able to see you," Nick answered smoothly, sitting down at the other end of the couch. "But should I be worried about you up there alone, Roxie?"

"I'll be fine." She waved off his concern, her eyes avoiding his. She didn't know if she'd be fine or not, but she didn't want to think about that right now.

"I'd feel better if you'd take a gun with you," he started, but the way she shook her head vehemently made him stop. "Why not?"

"Bringing a gun is just asking for something to happen," she replied, which made him shake his head. Only he added an eye-roll to his response.

"No, Roxie, it's not. It's being safe. Like wearing a condom, even if the woman isn't ovulating. Just in case..." he noticed the way her eyes narrowed, and her lips pursed and stopped with a sigh. "Fine, but I would feel better."

"I appreciate that, and your concern, but I can't go to New York with a gun. I'll call you if I need something when I'm there," she said to appease him.

"I hope you'll call me whether you need something or not, just to keep me updated." His voice came out smooth, but there was still worry there and that made her feel guilty.

But she'd carried around enough guilt for long

enough. It was time to get rid of some of it, and that meant facing her past, head-on. She couldn't do that here, even if it would be dangerous to go back home. "I'll call you every night, or send a message. I promise."

"That'll have to do, I guess. The car is here, are you ready?" Nick asked and Roxie got up.

"Yeah, I'm ready." She grabbed her bag from the floor where she'd dropped it and went for the door. "Are you coming with me?"

"No, I need to get some work done here, but if you need anything, just buzz me." He got up and followed her to the door, his hand coming to rest, not on her face, where it hovered for a moment, but on the edge of the door. "Let me know when you land. I'll be waiting."

"I will. Thanks, Nick." She pushed up to kiss his cheek lightly before she moved away. "I do appreciate it."

"It's my pleasure, Rox. Take care." His eyes clouded with sadness, but she watched it slip away into a smile.

"You too," she said and walked away from him, ready to get this all over with.

The car took her to the airport where she boarded Nick's private jet immediately. There was barely time for anyone that may have followed the car to recognize her, but just in case, she'd put on a hoodie to hide her hair. Once the plane landed and came to a stop, Roxie got out of her seat, bag over her shoulder, and walked off the plane.

She jumped in a taxi waiting outside the airport. The female driver entered the address Roxie had mentioned into a map app and then put the car in drive.

It wasn't long before memories from a decade before were nudged back to life. The oak tree at the junction of the road that would either take her to what used to be her home, or further down to what used to be June's home, still stood alive and well. It was huge and sprawling, full of secrets and silent memories that would never be spoken. Then the old green barn that still hadn't fallen down, in an abandoned lot, came into view, which caused a smile to pull at her lips.

She'd expected an empty lot where the house used to be, but as the driver drove up the driveway, Roxie was surprised to see a home that was just as sprawling as her old home had been filling the space. This home was brick, with three floors, but didn't sprawl out the way her old home had. Instead, the house was compact but still a mansion. Who lived there now? She wondered. Did they have a little girl who loved ballet so much that her parents built her a studio to practice in?

Were there many children in this new house, filling the place with laughter and warmth? Was there a pool in the back now, or a tennis court? What had replaced the things that had remained in her memory?

"Is this your final destination, miss?" The driver asked, not rushing her, but obviously needing to get on to the next ride, if Roxie was done.

"No, it's not, I just wanted to see this place first," Roxie said, before giving the driver another address.

This time, when they reached their destination, Roxie got out of the car. "Thanks for the ride."

"My pleasure. You take care," the driver said before Roxie closed the door.

The car drove off with the noise that comes from streets coated in fresh rain, but Roxie didn't notice. A glowing sign bordered by brick posts told her this was the Bennet Medical Group's hospital and outpatient service center. June worked here, as did her brother, Liam, and her father. Well, worked here, owned the place, whatever.

Roxie walked in through automatic doors and headed for the well-placed map on the wall at the entrance. She found June's office and headed up to the third floor to look for her friend. A receptionist there informed Roxie that June was not available so Roxie did something she wasn't sure she should do.

She'd seen Liam's name on that map and knew his office was just down from June's. A lot of time had passed since she'd last seen Liam, life had changed dramatically, and she'd become someone totally different from who she'd planned to be when she used to write her name as *Mrs. Liam Bennet* or *Mrs. Chloe Bennet* in her diary. Did he even look the same? She wondered as she waited for him in the reception area.

"Chloe?" Liam's surprised voice brought her eyes up from staring at a painting of a sailboat on the opposite wall.

He hadn't changed much at all; he'd just grown more handsome, she noticed immediately. Lincoln's step-brother had always looked different, with dark blond hair and bright green eyes being one of the major differences between them. Both were handsome men, but Liam's face was softer, not as solid as Lincoln's was. Liam still took care of himself, she felt, when he scooped her up into a hug, solid and firm muscles rippled beneath her hands.

"I can't believe you're here. I thought you were gone forever," Liam gushed, his eyes bright with happiness. "June told me you were back but it's one thing knowing and another thing seeing. Wow, you look great."

Roxie couldn't help but smile at his praise, but she felt embarrassed as the female receptionist looked on, murdering Roxie with the daggers in her eyes. Roxie pulled away, a smile replacing the frown she'd sent to the receptionist. "You look great too, you know?"

"Nah, I'm just me," he brushed off her praise and held his arm out to the door he'd walked out of. "Come to my office."

Roxie sent one final look back at the receptionist, still throwing daggers at her with those jealous brown eyes, and followed Liam. She hated when women acted like that, but she was too tired to rein in her small petty streak. "So, you're a doctor now?"

"Yeah, June and I both followed in dad's footsteps. Lincoln was the only one who managed to escape that little cliché." Liam showed her to a small brown sofa before he sat at the other end. It was definitely more inviting than sitting her in a chair in front of his desk and she felt at ease immediately. Even if she had once joined his name with hers. Roxie could feel heat flooding her cheeks at the reminder, but ignored it.

"It's not a cliché if you're making good money and helping people," she countered with a polite smile of admiration.

She was surprised, but that teenage infatuation seemed to be gone. Yeah, he was handsome, but he wasn't Lincoln, and something told her he was far too tame for her. It was probably the white button-up shirt under his lab coat, or the plain brown loafers on his feet that told her that. His outfit was expensive, sure, but those were most definitely plain loafers.

Too vanilla.

"I suppose you're right. Listen, are you in town for a while? I have surgery later, but then I'll be back at the old family home if you'd like to meet me there. Where are you staying?" He bombarded her with questions, but his smiling eyes didn't change a bit.

"Yeah, I haven't decided where I'm staying yet, I'm not sure how long I'll be in town, but I'd love to meet with you later. Can you let someone at the house know I'm coming?" She responded, trying to keep the questions straight as she answered.

"Of course, I'll let dad and my future stepmother know you're coming. I'm not sure if June is around this week, but she'll be happy to see you if she's in town. Our schedules make it hard to see each other. But yeah, dad will be excited you're back too. Wow, I can't believe you're back." He seemed agitated, but in a good way, and that made Roxie feel like she'd made the right decision in coming to see Liam.

He might tell Lincoln she was in town, which would give away her whole plan, but what could she do about it now? Not a lot.

Besides, it was really nice to see Liam again, even if it seemed her crush on the man had fizzled out. She'd had a crush on the boy and this man wasn't that boy anymore. She wasn't the girl who'd thought she was in love with him anymore either.

2

Roxie

L iam's dad had a new fiancé, her brain finally reminded her once she was standing in front of Dr. Bennet's house, her finger poised over the doorbell. Was the woman matronly and nice? Or was she the young, snotty, and resentful of her future stepchildren kind? Roxie hoped she was nice, as someone came to the door and opened it.

"You must be Chloe, come in." The older woman with long steel-gray hair, her eyes bright gray smiled at Roxie. She was probably in her late 50s but wore it well, Roxie decided. "I'm Olivia, George's fiancé. Liam called me to ask if I'd meet you here. Come on in."

Roxie blinked for a moment, trying to remember who George was before it dawned on her. Right, George

Bennet, June and Liam's dad. Roxie stepped into the house and memories immediately flooded through her mind. The millions of times she walked, or ran in, with June, so they could escape to June's room and talk about boys or their classmates in secret. The holidays they'd spent together, here and at Chloe's, the night she almost kissed Liam, all came flooding back into Roxie's mind.

Roxie smiled at the other woman and held out her hand as the memories began to fade and reality came back to her. "Sorry, I wasn't expecting to be hit with a walk down memory lane. Yes, I'm Chloe, Chloe Abshire."

The name felt wrong on Roxie's lips, foreign somehow, the name unfamiliar and alien. Still, that name was who she was for the first eighteen years of her life, it was what Liam and George Bennet knew her as, and using anything else with them would seem strange. June would use the name she'd taken, if June was in town, but that would be alright. It would all get explained somewhere along the way.

"You're an old friend of June's?" Olivia asked as she walked in the direction of the room the family had always used as the family living room. There was a more formal sitting room, or used to be, for visitors, so Roxie was glad when the woman took her to the non-formal family area. It meant she respected Roxie's place in the family.

"I am, we used to be inseparable, really." Roxie looked around as she walked, noting the changes made over the last ten years, and wondered if that was from the divorce, when Ms. Young left Mr. Bennet, or if that was just the sign of time passing. Probably both, Roxie decided, as she took a leather wingback chair as a seat.

"I see. Will you be staying here with the kids? George and I don't live here, I just came over to make sure someone was here to meet you, since Liam asked," Olivia asked politely, without judgment in her eyes. Roxie liked her already.

"I, well, I don't know. I hadn't got that far yet," she answered honestly, feeling at ease with the woman immediately. "This was kind of an impulsive trip, and I'm sorry, I haven't got everything straight yet."

"It's no problem. Only Liam and June keep bedrooms here now, the rest are all open to guests, anytime, especially old friends. Let me know and we'll get you sorted out later. Are you hungry or thirsty?"

Roxie settled into the chair while Olivia went to get her a glass of tea. She would have looked at her phone, but she'd have to turn it on, and she knew what would happen if she did. It would probably vibrate to death from Lincoln's calls and messages. Best save that for later and figure out what she was going to do now that she was back in New York.

This might not have been one of her best ideas. Too

late for second thoughts now, though, she decided, as Olivia came back in with a tray. She was here and she'd better do what she came to do. Somehow. It might have been better to stay in South Carolina, to go to Lincoln's and let this all go, but she needed closure of some kind. She wouldn't get that in South Carolina, waiting on answers to magically appear.

"Here we are." Olivia handed her a glass of iced tea before she picked up a cup of what looked like coffee. A very expensive porcelain one, Roxie noted when Olivia lifted the white, black, and gold cup with a Rosenthal Versace stamp on the bottom to her lips. Her mother had owned a similar set before the house burned down.

Sadness nearly took her breath away, the memory of her mother using those cups startling her abruptly.

"Oh, my dear, what's wrong?" Olivia asked with kindness, putting the cup down with care.

"Nothing, I'm sorry." Roxie turned her head away, trying to catch her breath and blink away the tears. "I have a lot of memories in this house, and well, I guess you don't know, but my parents died in a fire not far from here. We had a lovely home, and I haven't been back here since that night. In fact, I was here when the house caught on fire…"

Roxie's words trailed off, knowing she was spilling private information to a virtual stranger. She wasn't normally this open, but Olivia exuded comfort like a warm home on a cold night. Roxie blinked the last of the tears away and smiled with a confidence she didn't feel.

"That's terrible, I'm so sorry to hear that." The tranquility in Olivia's voice soothed Roxie's rattled and bruised nerves. "I remember George mentioning something about that when we were out on a drive one night. You're the girl who disappeared?"

Roxie's eyebrows lifted, astonished that Mr. Bennet remembered her and had spoken about her. He'd always been nice to her, but that he'd even thought about her told her he'd cared more than she thought. Knowing that warmed her heart and made her glad she'd come back.

"I am, yes. It's complicated, but I had my reasons. That's why I came back, I'm at a point in my life where I need answers, and the only place I'll get them is here." Roxie shrugged, her words trailing off as she tried to decide what else she could say without making Olivia uncomfortable.

Roxie liked the older woman in a way she hadn't experienced before. Trusting people hadn't come easy to her since her parents' deaths, but Olivia was different, and Roxie knew that instinctively.

Olivia picked her cup back up and smiled easily at Roxie. "He'll be really glad you're back then. And I'm sure he'll help in any way he can. George is resourceful, after all."

"He always was," Roxie agreed, picking up her glass and settling back into her chair. "He was always so gentle with everyone around him and determined to make sure people were comfortable. I always thought it was because he was a doctor, but doctors now seem more bent on making sure their patients don't bother them than putting them at ease."

"George is always a doctor, but that doesn't make him cold like some of his associates. He's a different breed, I guess. Surgeons can be arrogant and rude, but he's the exact opposite." Olivia smiled a smile that was a mixture of inner peace and pleasure at the thought of the man it was now obvious she loved.

Roxie was glad to see that maybe the older man had found love at long last. Lincoln's mother was a hard woman to love, but even Roxie had seen that Mr. Bennet had loved her. It was good to know he'd found a woman like Olivia to share his life with. If only Roxie could find that same kind of peace with Lincoln.

No, you aren't thinking about him right now, she chided herself and put the glass of tea down. "He's a very kind man."

That seemed a lame statement, but it was true.

"He is." Olivia nodded, the conversation was about to become awkward but Olivia inhaled and changed directions. "I have to go out for a little while, but feel free to make yourself at home."

"Oh, well, maybe I'll go for a walk then," Roxie replied with a polite smile, not sure of what else she should say.

Roxie hadn't expected to be left in the house on her own, but it seemed Olivia had made a judgment that meant the unknown younger woman wouldn't rob her of her possessions. That was nice too, being trusted like that. Of course, Liam had called ahead so maybe he'd reassured Olivia that Roxie was to be trusted.

Either way, Roxie was at loose ends now with nothing to do. She'd suggested she'd take a walk, so perhaps that's just what she would do.

"Just leave your glass there, the maid will pick it up. I really do hate to leave you, but I have an appointment I can't miss. If you need anything, or decide you will be staying the night, just let the maid know and she'll get you settled. She's normally in the kitchen at this time of day, but if you can't find her, just press the top button on the white panel by the front door and it will call her. The door is unlocked, so you're free to come and go as you please." Olivia stood up as she spoke, her mind obviously on whatever her next task was. She clasped her hands and focused on Roxie once more. "It's been really lovely to meet you and I hope you do decide to stay, I know George would be pleased if you did, Chloe."

That name jarred her again, but Roxie hid it with a

bland smile. "Thank you, Olivia, I may just do that. I hope everything goes well with your appointment."

"Thank you, Chloe. I'll see you soon." Olivia gave a slight nod of her head before she headed out of the room.

Roxie sat there, trying to adjust to being called that name again. It wasn't easy, hearing it like that, even though she knew it was her name and it had been used often lately. Still, that wasn't who she was now, though that would be hard to explain to those who used to know her.

When the front door closed and a car zoomed away, Roxie got up and looked around the house. She found everything familiar, but somehow different. Time and Olivia had changed most of the decor. Why she'd expected the house to look exactly the same, she couldn't imagine. Well, it was her imagination that did that, wasn't it? She'd kept the house the same in her mind all these years, even if she knew things would probably have changed. That's how the past was, houses, people, places stayed the same, until you visited them all again and found out everything had changed.

Sunlight streaming through the windows drew her outside to walk around the grounds. The pool was still there, even if the furniture around it was changed. Where there used to be teal and purple cushions, there were now colors Roxie would call oatmeal and almond decorating the umbrellas, tables, and chairs. There was even new paint on the pool house, gone was the dark wood stain, now replaced with a light stain that lifted the mood around the place.

A further walk revealed a new stable with six horses inside. Roxie wasn't sure which of the family members was into horses, but it was obvious one of them was. The horses were topnotch, well-bred animals, judging by their shiny coats and striking features. She didn't know much about horses, but she did know the difference between a plow horse and a thoroughbred.

Roxie left the stable and headed in a familiar direction, the path that would lead her home. She paused, noting that the birdhouse had been replaced along with the fence. Stone stood in the place of wood and the birdhouse was now a marble griffin. Another sign of time passing, she thought, her fingers tracing over the griffin. It was doubtful Mr. Bennet had any idea how important that birdhouse was to Liam and Roxie, but still, she was sad to see it was gone.

Everything seemed smaller as she walked up the road and turned down the road that would take her to where the house she'd lived in used to be. She hadn't meant to walk down to the place, her feet had brought her here from muscle memory alone. From her short trip earlier, she knew that the house had been replaced, there was no sign of the old place, really, just that old tree and not much else. She didn't go into the grounds, she didn't want to trespass, especially when she could see no real sign that anyone else had ever lived there, no indication that another house was once here, before it burned to the ground.

She wondered if anything at the back of the house was still the same, but didn't dare cross the driveway to find out. There were no cars up front, but that didn't mean anything. There might be someone home who would allow her to walk around and seek out signs of what used to be, but sense took over before she could embarrass herself like that.

The lost house was another part of the past that could not be brought back to life. She wanted to continue to look around but decided that she'd had enough for the day. She'd run away from Lincoln, from the future which looked far too bleak, and come back here looking for answers. There were no guarantees she'd get any answers, but she knew she'd never find a clue about what had happened if she kept spending all of her time here waltzing through the past.

That made her smile as she turned from the house and headed back to the Bennet residence. Waltzing through the past indeed. She always had some form of dance on her mind. Even now, when she had nowhere to dance. It wasn't likely there was a studio here for June, the girl had grown up to become a woman in medical school and then a doctor. Roxie doubted June did very much ballet anymore, if she did manage to find spare time.

Roxie spoke with the maid when she got back inside the house and asked for a room. When the woman opened the door that used to be Lincoln's room, Roxie wondered if fate really hated her that much. Still, she thanked the woman for her assistance and threw her bag on the bed.

There wasn't much in the bag; pajamas, necessities, her handbag, another pair of jeans, and a few shirts, but nothing fancy. She hadn't planned to stay long, and she hadn't planned to do much more than visit the police station that had investigated the deaths of her parents and the fire. After that, she didn't know what else she could do, but she was determined to do something.

There was a television in the room, so she turned it on, found a movie, and watched it while she waited for the family to come home. Liam arrived first, knocking at her door.

"Laura told me she'd put you in here. Is everything alright? Do you need anything?" Liam asked from the door, not coming into the room. He'd always been a gentleman.

"No, I'm fine," Roxie said and shook her head no. "What are you doing now?"

"I thought I'd have a drink after I change, if you'd like

to join me?" Liam asked, his hand still on the doorknob as if to keep him safe from falling into the room.

Roxie couldn't help the smile that idea gave her, and agreed to a drink. "Just let me know when you're ready."

"Of course." Liam nodded and closed the door softly.

He'd always been gentle and quiet, not loud and boisterous like his friends. That was one of the things that had drawn her attention all those years ago. Fifteen minutes later, Liam knocked at the door, with wet hair and dressed in a black polo shirt and khaki trousers. "Ready?"

"Yes, thank you." Roxie scooted off the bed to follow him down the stairs and to a sitting room decorated in dark woods and masculine earth tones. This must have been decorated by Liam himself, or by Mr. Bennet.

"Have a seat." Liam indicated an antique leather sofa while he went to a drinks cabinet. "What will you have?"

"Just some water, please, Liam," she answered, not interested in alcohol at that moment.

"Are you sure? There's juice as well," he offered but she refused it. "Here's your water then."

"Thanks. So, you still live here?"

"Yes, sometimes. I have an apartment closer to the hospital, but I like to come back here when I can. There's no place like home, right?" He grinned at her as he took a seat in a dark leather armchair to her left.

"I suppose. It's been a long time since I've been

home." She smiled weakly and sipped at the glass of water he'd poured her. "I see the fence was replaced with a stone wall. Do you remember the birdhouse that used to be there?"

She wasn't sure why she asked, whether to prompt his memory about what they used to mean to each other, or just out of curiosity, but the words were out before she could stop them.

"I think so, yes. I'm not sure who put it there or why. We never put birdfeed in it, and I never saw a bird near it. I think it was too exposed for any bird families to move in." His smile was charming but devoid of any memory associated with letters or the secret words he'd written to her.

No matter, she decided, even if she had kept the last letter he'd written to her. Lincoln had replaced all of the men in her life, as if he'd stamped himself all over her to warn other men away. At least, that's how she felt when she thought about it. Even if he was done with her, she still felt like she belonged to him, despite how she'd run away.

"Does your wife or girlfriend plan to come to dinner tonight?" She asked him, wondering if there was someone special in his life.

Liam smiled a smile so charming it nearly disarmed before he even spoke. "No, I'm not seeing anyone at the moment. No wife, no boyfriends either, before you ask."

His wink told her he was teasing her, making her smile with a soft laugh. "Well, things change. I miss how simple and innocent life used to be sometimes, but I wouldn't be bothered if you had a boyfriend, you know? It wouldn't shock me, I mean."

Now she was flubbing again.

"I'm sure it wouldn't, but no, I like women. In fact, I wish I'd had the courage to tell you how much I liked you before you disappeared, but I never could get the nerve up." Liam took a drink of his scotch before he put the glass down on a coaster and looked at her.

Roxie frowned, confused. But he had told her, in every letter he wrote to her. Maybe he just meant he regretted not saying it to her face. Oh well, it was all in the past now anyway.

"All water under the bridge, now," Roxie said finally, knowing that Liam could never replace Lincoln in her heart. It was a pity, but that was just the fact.

3

Roxie

"Oh, dad's arrived," Liam said softly, the moment gone already.

Roxie frowned, but then let it go. It was probably best not to dig up her past with him, anyway. She was in love with his brother, jerk that he was, so anything that might have been with Liam was long gone.

"Chloe," Dr. Bennet breathed out in shock when she walked into the hallway to greet him. "I know the kids said you were here, but I still couldn't quite believe it. It's so good to see you."

Roxie smiled at the man who'd grown older, like everybody else she used to know. His hair was more gray than black now, and there were deep lines around his eyes, where there used to be slight indentations. His eyes were still bright and full of concern, however, and she walked into his open arms with relief.

It felt good to get a hug from him, like she was almost really home again.

"It's good to see you too, Dr. Bennet," Roxie said as the hug went on. She didn't want to let go, she felt so safe, but knew she had to. "How have you been?"

"I've been fine, honey. How are you?" His dark brown eyes examined her from head to toe and she was pleased when he didn't frown at her choice of hair color. "You look great. Healthy."

"Yes, I stay active with work and the dance classes I teach," she replied, though she didn't go into what kind of dance she taught.

"That's good. Are you staying long?" He nodded his head towards a sofa, and she joined him there.

"I'm not sure yet. I have some questions I need to get answers to, about the, well, the fire that killed my parents." She held his gaze and saw that he seemed to know that was what she'd say.

"I expected you to show up looking for those answers if you were able to." He nodded again, his eyes moving to the window. "I bought the property from your father just before his death, did you know that?"

"What?" Roxie looked at the older man with a frown of surprise. "No, I didn't know that. Why would they sell the house to you? I don't understand."

Dr. Bennet took Roxie's hand with a sigh of sympathy. "Well, since you were accepted into the ballet school in Paris, they decided to relocate there. They wouldn't have needed the house here…"

His words trailed off as her jaw dropped and her eyes went wide. "I was accepted into the ballet school?"

"Yes, they were planning to surprise you with the news, but, well, the fire happened. Then you disappeared. Lincoln and I have been looking for you ever since. You see, I'm also the executor of their wills," Dr. Bennet paused, gathering his thoughts before he spoke again. "You have an inheritance, you know?"

"No, I didn't know," Roxie murmured, her mind whirling in disbelief. Too much information had been dumped in the few sentences he'd spoken to her. "I was accepted into the ballet school?"

She couldn't help but go back to the one thing that had mattered to her so much back then. It was almost cruel, but she knew her parents had only wanted to surprise her. That knowledge could have changed everything, though. She could have gone off to Paris to live her life, learning French, dating French men, honing her ballet skills. It would have been the perfect place to hide all of these years.

But then she wouldn't have her daughter. She wouldn't have the independence she had now. She wouldn't know just how strong she was, well, maybe she would have learned all of that, but the fact remained, she had a daughter now that would not have been born if she'd known she'd been accepted into the ballet school in France. She may have still slept with Lincoln that night, but her choices would have been a lot different.

Roxie felt the weight of the world settle on her shoulders and the sensation of being strangled made her reach for her neck.

"Breathe Chloe. Come on, don't panic on me." Dr. Bennet gripped her right hand, taking it from her throat to pat it, to bring her back from the edge by focusing on him.

"I can't breathe," she garbled out around her tight throat, wanting to wrap her own hand around her neck again.

"You can, honey. In, out. In, out." He set the rhythm and she followed, trusting him to lead her in the right direction.

"There's an inheritance?" She asked when she felt almost human again.

"Yes, your parents had some money, a few safe deposit boxes at the bank, and some properties that they did not sell. If you're careful with it all, you won't ever have to work again. Of course, I don't know what's in the safe deposit boxes, I've left them alone, but there may be a lot in them that you'll want." Dr. Bennet's voice tapered off as panic threatened to overwhelm her again.

She didn't want to accept money that had come about because her parents died, but at the same time… she would be more independent if she didn't have to work, if she could provide for her daughter without Lincoln's help. She could get custody of her, buy a nice house, send her to good schools, everything Lincoln could do. They'd be, for the first time since they'd met again, on equal footing.

"Do you remember you have an aunt in Paris?" Dr. Bennet asked, but Roxie shook her head.

"No, not that I remember." Roxie searched her memory, but couldn't remember either of her parents having siblings or even aunts and uncles. "Who is she?"

"She's related to you through your father. She wanted to take over your inheritance, but your father made an iron-clad will. He may have wanted to change it, but I have a feeling he would have given the rights over to her if that's what he'd actually wanted. Anyway, I had a feeling you'd be back, even if she wanted to have you declared dead, so I've kept everything intact for your return. And here you are." He held his hands out in wonder and Roxie couldn't hold back the smile his happy face brought to life on hers.

"Thank you, Dr. Bennet. That means a lot to me. Even if my aunt seems like a horrible old cow." Roxie grinned and took a deep breath, relaxing at last. "Wow, I had no idea about any of this. So I've learned a few things already that I wished I'd known back then."

Dr. Bennet nodded and it finally occurred to Roxie that he'd said he'd bought the property where the house used to be. "So is that your house over there?"

"Yes, I live there with Olivia. This house is full of memories of the kids when they were children, and of… well, the past." Dr. Bennet stopped and Roxie had a feeling he was thinking about Lincoln's mother. He'd really loved her, even if he'd let her go. "It belongs to them all now. Would you like to see the house I built there? I can take you by tomorrow."

"That would be great," she replied, although she wasn't sure it would be that at all. It would probably be weird, being in a place that should be familiar but wasn't. It wouldn't feel like the same house, even if the rooms had all been rebuilt in the exact same way. It couldn't feel the same, she'd never lived in that new house. But, still, it would be nice to see what had replaced her old home.

"Tomorrow, then. Tonight we'll have dinner here and let you relive the past. I'll have to clear my schedule," he said absently and got out his phone. "I'll need to go by the bank with you, do you have an ID with you?"

"I have my license and social security card." She lifted one shoulder with a frown. "But that's, um, well, in my new name."

"Ah, I see. Okay, well, there may be some documents in the safe deposit boxes at the bank that will help me transfer everything over to you. Don't worry. If not, we can get my lawyer to settle everything. I may need to call him anyway. Let me see."

Dr. Bennet stabbed at his phone with his index finger, typed in a message to someone, sent it off, but then he moved, and Roxie couldn't see what he was doing anymore. It gave her time to think, to ponder over whether she wanted to reclaim her old, original identity or not. She'd have to in order to claim her inheritance, but then there'd be questions she didn't really want to answer from other places. This could bring her trouble.

"Maybe we should talk to that lawyer first, Dr. Bennet?" Roxie said softly, not sure how to broach the subject.

"Oh, because you have a different identity now? Yes, we're taking care of that, June explained it all to me this morning." Dr. Bennet's smile was full of pride when he looked up from his phone. "That was awfully clever of you, changing your identity."

"Well, I recognized two of the men who were talking to the fire department that night. They'd been to the house before, and I knew they were trouble. I think the fire was deliberate, even if the cops think it was murder/suicide."

"I always thought the same, myself. I just couldn't

figure out who would be the culprit. Your father was never a shady kind of man. He was always respectable, and so in love with his family that he wouldn't do anything to jeopardize any of you." Dr. Bennet stopped, inhaled, and lifted his eyebrows. "Anyway, for now, let's focus on getting to know each other again, shall we? We can do adulting tomorrow. Isn't that what you kids all say now?"

His grin was as white and bright as it had always been, and just as infectious. Roxie let her dark thoughts of doom and gloom slip away as she smiled. Of course, Dr. Bennet already had a lawyer working to fix any problem she might have when it came to claiming her inheritance. Like Lincoln, he was a problem-solver, a take-charge kind of man who would never let his friends or family worry if he could help it.

She'd barely been back in town a few hours and already problems were being solved, answers being given, and she was about to step back into a life she thought she'd left behind. Being Chloe again wasn't something she'd ever planned to do, but she might have to be that girl for a little while, in order to go back to her life as Roxie.

It was all giving her a headache, so she stood up and followed Dr. Bennet into the dining room with Liam.

"June is on her way," Liam said after he picked up his phone and then put it down. "She won't be long."

"We'll wait for her then. Hello, darling." Dr. Bennet turned to face Olivia as she came into the room. She took the place to his left at the table, with Liam to his right. Roxie was beside Liam and sipped at a glass filled with water. It was strange to see the pair together, despite the years that had passed.

Roxie knew Lincoln's mother was no longer in the picture, but in her mind, they'd spent all of these years together, her and Dr. Bennet. To see another woman in Ms. Young's place was just…strange.

"Are you alright?" Liam bent towards her to ask quietly, prompting Roxie to nod.

"I'm fine, it's just all kind of surreal at the moment," she whispered. "I guess I wasn't expecting all of you to take me back with open arms. Or for things to have changed so much."

"Of course, we'd accept you back. You were like a part of this family. She and June were like sisters, always together, always whispering with each other," Dr. Bennet said, speaking in turn to Roxie and Olivia after overhearing the conversation.

"I can't thank you enough, Dr. Bennet, for every-thing." Roxie smiled at him, feeling what must have been a glow in her eyes and on her face. She felt as if she'd come home, in a way. And when June breezed into the dining room, swooping Roxie into a huge hug, that feeling solidified into happiness.

"I'm so glad you're here. I took the rest of the evening off, don't worry, Dad, I made sure all my patients were good before I left," June said, and Roxie caught the bemused smile on his face just before he spoke.

"I have complete faith in you, June, you know that," he answered with a smile of pleasure at his daughter. "Your patients always come first."

It was good to be back.

4

Roxie

*R*oxie woke up to the smell of coffee in her temporary room, and a smiling June bouncing on the bed. When they were kids, she'd wake up to find hot chocolate on the nightstand with a much younger June bouncing just like she was now. The sweetness of it all made Roxie smile as she reached for her friend.

"Good morning," she said with a wan smile. "What time is it?"

"It's almost 8:30, and I couldn't wait anymore. Remember this?" June thrust a box at Roxie just as Roxie pushed herself up in the bed.

Roxie's eyes went round, the box was one of the most

familiar things she'd seen in a long time. "Your ballet box! You kept it?"

It was a plastic bin that June had decorated when they were about eight, a bin that June used to hide her tutus and ballet shoes in. Liam and his friends had taken some of June's ballet stuff and all but destroyed it that summer, playing around in the backyard and the pool. It had made June so mad that she'd found the box and would hide it in different places every day to keep the boys from ever finding it again.

"Well, duh," June laughed, rolling her eyes. "I can't wear any of it anymore, but some of your stuff is in here too. I couldn't get rid of it. Especially when I thought I'd never see you again."

June's sob of pain and the way she hid her head were like a stab wound to Roxie. She took her friend in her arms and let her cry, trying to soothe her as she mumbled words Roxie couldn't quite make out. Roxie's eyes started to leak too, as June cried, her hand clenching at Roxie's arms. "It's okay, June, I'm right here."

"I knoooooow!" June wailed, sitting up a little to look at Roxie's face. "But for so long I didn't know. I missed you, I wished you'd come back into my life, I feared that you never would, but now you're here, and, oh my God, I'm crying all over you." June laughed at herself, grabbing a tissue from the box on the nightstand before she wiped at her face and blew her nose. "Sorry."

"Don't be, honey." Roxie blubbered a little herself and grabbed for one of the pink tissues that smelled like baby powder. "I should have found a way to let you know I was alright. I just didn't know how."

"And you were coping with far more than I could have dreamed of. Pregnancy, everything with your parents, being alone. It all must have been over-whelming and merely surviving must have taken all of your energy." June brushed aside anything that Roxie might have said and forgave her all at the same time.

It was something June had always done, forgiven easily, made excuses for others, found the reasons behind behaviors that many might not have accepted. She was too forgiving, maybe for her own good, Roxie thought now. "Yeah, all of that is true, but I still could have said something."

"Don't worry about it. Just get dressed and come with me. We're going out for breakfast. And you can keep the box if you want. Like I said, some of that stuff in there is yours. Outfits and shoes we outgrew, things like that." June got up and waited for Roxie to agree with a wide grin. "I'm not leaving until you agree."

"Oh, I see," Roxie said playfully, throwing the white duvet back from her legs. "Blackmail is the first order of the day?"

"Yes, my dear, it is. Now, are we going out to eat or not?" June bounced in place, obviously supremely happy to have her friend back in her life.

Roxie was happy to have June in hers, too. "Of course, we are, June! Just let me get ready and we'll go wherever you want."

"Good!" June cried, and danced out of the room on her tiptoes, the way she used to do when they were young.

Roxie showered, put on a pair of jeans and a black sweater, tied on a pair of black and white canvas shoes, and decided to go without makeup. Her black and purple hair was decoration enough for the morning, even if she looked about twelve without makeup on days like today. It didn't matter. She was only going out with June for breakfast. It wasn't like she was going on a date.

It did turn out the morning was a walk down memory lane, however.

June drove them into town, past the cemetery, prompting a question Roxie hadn't thought about until now. "Do you know where my parents are buried?"

June stiffened beside Roxie, her eyes leaving the road for a minute. "Yeah, want me to take you after breakfast?"

"I'm supposed to meet your dad at some point today, but he said he'd text you when he was ready for me. Yeah, that sounds like a plan." Roxie had left her phone off, not wanting to let Lincoln know where she was, if his family hadn't already told him without her knowing, that is.

"I can take you tomorrow if dad needs you after we eat." June smiled with reassurance at Roxie.

Roxie just nodded, suspecting where they were going.

"I had a feeling we were coming here," Roxie said when June pulled up in front of a familiar restaurant. "Mr. Parker's pancakes were always the best around."

"You remember? Awesome!" June said as they took a booth seat and gave their order to the waitress.

Roxie didn't bother to look at the menu, she knew what she wanted, the same thing Lincoln had brought to her that one day that seemed like so long ago. Only, it wasn't that long ago. She asked for coffee and orange juice before the waitress left.

"June! Where's Lincoln at?" Mr. Parker asked as he came out of the back with two plates piled high with pancakes, bacon, and sausage links. "Wait…Chloe?"

Roxie smiled up at the man, a little rounder and grayer with age, but still Mr. Parker. "Yeah, it's me, Mr. Parker."

"It's so good to see you. How are you?" He beamed at Roxie as he set the plates down on their table and stared at her in amazement. "You look great."

"Thanks." Roxie felt her cheeks going red and ducked

her head down. Her fingers brushed at the back of her neck, before she finally looked back up at him. "I'm good, how are you?"

"Great, even better to know you've come back. What a day! It's not even lunchtime yet and my day has been made. I'll let you eat. Enjoy it, girls." Mr. Parker moved away with a small wave and June grinned at Roxie.

"I knew he'd be excited to see you." June's brown eyes gleamed with tears, but she blinked them away. "He asked about you for the longest time, but then he stopped one day. I guess it was painful and he knew it."

"I'm sorry," Roxie said, feeling the sorrow she expressed. "I guess I didn't know what I meant to everyone here."

"You meant a lot to a lot of people. You still do. Now, let's eat and not start off a crying jag again, alright?"

"Yep, sounds like a plan." Roxie picked up her fork and dug in.

The taste of pancakes covered in fresh-cut strawberries and maple syrup was too much to resist and Roxie ate everything on her plate. "These are as good as I remember."

It was even better than the treat Lincoln had brought to her as a surprise, but that was only because this plate of food was fresh. Roxie would have told June about that surprise, but it was personal, a moment she'd shared with Lincoln that she didn't want to share with anyone else but him. And right now, she didn't want to think about him at all, so it was time to do something else.

"Has your dad pinged you?" Roxie asked, prompting June to look at her phone.

"Not yet, no. Shall I drive you over there now? I'll have to head in to work after, but we can fit a quick trip in. If that's alright?" June looked kind of like she'd said something wrong, but Roxie waved it off.

"I know you're busy, June. I can get a cab over and back to the house if you need me to?" Roxie offered, not wanting June to feel guilty.

"No, it's fine, I think," June said, but her smile was tight. June would never admit she was inwardly panicking about being on time, but Roxie knew her friend, even if ten years had passed.

She'd be quick at the cemetery, then, to make sure June got to work on time. Only, she didn't anticipate how seeing the gravestone would make her feel. As she looked down at her mother and father's names on the single headstone in the sprawling cemetery, grief surged to life.

It came over her like a heart-wrenching tidal wave, nearly knocking her to her knees. She'd grieved over the years, in bursts, when she had time, but nothing like this. It was like a dam bursting, and it was all she could do to breathe in and out.

"Oh, Roxie, I'm so sorry." June embraced Roxie in a

tight hug. Roxie wrapped her arms around June's small waist and tried to stop the outflow. Nothing worked though, no matter how hard she tried to swallow the tears. Time ticked by and Roxie eventually pulled away, to tell her friend to get to work, despite the grief that still stung at the old wound as though it were still new and raw.

"I think I want to stay here for a while, if that's okay? I'll walk back into town and catch a cab. No, really, go to work, I'll be fine." Roxie stopped June's protests with a frown. "I need some time here, more than I thought. You get off to work. Really."

"I don't like this, but I do have patients I need to check on this morning. Here, take this phone, it's a spare I keep for personal use." June dug around in her purse until she pulled out an older generation iPhone. "It's been off, but it's charged, so you'll be good to go. There's a number for the local taxi in there."

"Thanks, June. I appreciate it." Roxie dropped the phone in her bag and grabbed a tissue. "I'll be fine. Go on."

"Okay, I'll buzz you later." June looked around, maybe for someone to stay with Roxie, but the place was empty at this time of day, except for a small funeral taking place at the other end of the cemetery, so far away that Roxie could barely see the people standing around an open grave.

"That's fine." Roxie leaned over, kissed June's cheek, and then shooed her away. "Go on now."

"See you later." June waved, then turned to walk away. Roxie watched, saw June turn back, and waved at her to tell her to go one more time.

Finally, she was alone with her parents, well, as alone as you could be with a cemetery as full as this one. "I'm sorry it's taken me so long to find you two."

Roxie sank down to the ground and traced the letters on the gravestone. One line underneath their names nearly tore Roxie's heart open.

We will always miss you, Chloe.

They were loved and respected. Roxie knew that because Dr. Bennet had made sure their wishes were respected. They must have chosen that sentence knowing that she would come back to them one day, here, without them in the real world. Of all of their accomplishments in life, of all the things they could have boasted about on their gravestone, they'd chosen to let their daughter, and the world, know that she was loved just as much as they were.

Tears streamed out of her eyes and her nose was running, but the deep sobs of grief had passed. "You have a granddaughter, you know? Her name is Lily and she's so beautiful and smart. Like her dad in many ways, but so many things about her remind me of you two as well."

Roxie paused, pulling her lips in to try to stop another sob. "You know her dad, Lincoln Young. We made her together, on the night you died. I didn't know what to do, I was so afraid, but she was this spark that I couldn't get rid of. I wondered when Dr. Bennet told me that I'd been accepted into the Paris Ballet Academy if I'd have chosen differently when it came to her, but now? Now, I know I'd have kept her. I needed a part of you two with me, and she is that. A part of you, me, and her dad. I think I made the right choice, knowing what I do now."

Roxie brushed at her face with another tissue and tried to smile. "This is kind of strange, talking to you like this, but I think you can hear me. I hope you can anyway. I know you two were wrapped up in each other, but despite that, you still made me feel loved and I miss that so much. I haven't allowed myself to think about it really, because it hurts so much, what happened to you. But I want you to know, I haven't wasted my life. It hasn't turned out the way I planned for it to, but it hasn't been wasted. And I won't ever waste a moment of it, I promise you that. I'll find the people responsible for your deaths, somehow, and I'll make sure they pay."

The one-sided conversation had gone a little dark there, but it wasn't like anyone was around to hear her. Roxie heard a twig snap and looked around. There wasn't anyone about, not that she could see, so she put it down to a cat or squirrel.

"I'll make sure you two are always proud of me, no matter what I do with my life," she said at last, and got up from the ground. "I'll come back before I go back to Myrtle Beach."

She touched the gravestone and held her fingers there for a lingering moment. It was as near to her parents as she'd ever get again. She wanted to hold onto them for just a moment longer.

5

Roxie

"Where the fuck am I?" Roxie demanded to know as soon as the gag was removed, but a bottle of water was shoved into her mouth right away, cutting off her words with sharp pain. The lid of the bottle pushed her lip into her teeth and she tasted blood with the water. *Asshole.*

But she only thought the word at the guy, without actually saying it. They wore black balaclavas, black clothes, and kept their faces turned away as often as possible. She knew they were the two that had snuck up on her because she could smell the gallons of cheap cologne one of them had on. It was so awful it nearly took her breath away, but at least the rag they'd tied around her head was gone now.

She'd nearly gagged when she woke up to find her mouth filled with cloth, but the terror had soon replaced the sick feeling. One minute she'd been looking around at the cemetery, the next she smelled that horrible cologne and felt something pierce her skin. They'd drugged her with something to knock her out. She knew that because she'd woken up in the back of a van moving down the road.

When the van stopped, the two men opened the doors, one with a gun trained on her while the other dragged her out of the back. That guy had thrown her over his shoulder to carry her to a chair. He'd tied her to that chair with twists of rope around her body, down to where he'd wrapped the rope not around the back of the chair, but the chair legs. She wasn't getting out of all that rope easily.

Everything was kind of jumbled together now, and her cheeks were bruised. She'd tried to ask questions, but every question had resulted in a slap that stung and made her ears ring. She'd stopped asking after a while, but had hoped they'd mellowed a little as time passed. Obviously not.

She was afraid but would be damned if she'd show it. She'd looked around the empty apartment, but it was empty. Just bare white walls, a few strips of pine here and there, on the floor and the baseboards, but otherwise, no color. At least it was still sunny, so she could see what was going on. Though, as high up as it seemed they were, she didn't see a lot. Just the sky changing as the hours passed.

There were probably things she should say, that Lincoln would kill them all, or he'd pay them any ransom they wanted. That she didn't know what they wanted but she'd figure out how to get it to them. She didn't even know if their plan was ransom. They might be about to sell her to the highest bidder, for all she knew.

The two men, both over six feet tall, hadn't said a single word in her presence. They just glared at her questions, after one of them slapped her, of course, and kept their lips sealed.

She'd wanted to know who they were, who they worked for, and what they wanted, but there'd been no answers, only violence. A phone chirped on one of the duo and the not-stinky guy pulled it out to read the message. He showed it to the other guy, who looked over at her with a malicious smile.

Roxie's blood went cold and if she hadn't been so securely tied to the chair she might have started to shake. The circulation to her hands and feet was cut off, she was tied so tightly. Still, fear replaced her bravado of a moment ago, when she tried to ask another question and got a busted lip for it.

"Stop. You don't want to do anything to hurt me."

She tried to implore them with her eyes, but they weren't looking at her. They were too busy untying the yards of rope they'd wrapped her in. Which could only mean they were about to move her. Why? Were they planning to kill her? The stinky guy had the gun, it was in a shoulder holster.

If she could get her hands free, she might be able to grab the gun. Distract them. Questions seemed to piss them off, that would do the trick.

"Come on, guys. I know a lot of rich people. Tell me what you want, what I've done, how I can make whatever is wrong right, and I'll do what I can, really." She paused when the stinky guy stopped to glower at her. "Seriously now, dude. What have I done to you? Do you want money? I can get you money, just give me a phone, and I'll get you all the money you want."

Her answer was another slap, this one spun her head off to the right and she felt her bottom lip split. She gave a short scream of pain, but shut up after that. They weren't in charge, that was clear from that text message and what they were doing now, but she didn't want to die. Were they taking her off to kill her?

The not-stinky guy yanked her up, threw her over his shoulder, and carried her into a dark room. Mr. Stinky held up a flashlight to a length of chain that was secured to the wall. Her hands were tied in front of her so when not-stinky guy looped the chain around her waist she had to hold her hands up. The chain didn't hurt, it just added a weight she didn't want to feel. She could see from the length of the rope that she could walk around the room, and knew she wasn't leaving it when Mr. Stinky turned the beam of the flashlight to a bucket in a corner of the room.

Horror filled her as she realized what it was for, but she tried to look around, to find a way to escape. There was nothing in the room that could help her save herself though, not that she could see. Just a chain and a bucket.

The two men left her, with one of them patting her on the ass before they left. That made her skin crawl, but she was used to the unwanted touches of assholes like these two. She ignored the touch, as she had so many before. Before, she'd needed her job, so she hadn't broken the assholes' fingers. Now, she was tied up, she wouldn't be breaking anyone's anything.

Not-stinky guy came back in with a case of bottled water, put it just within her reach, then left. She heard the lock on the door click, much like the padlock they'd locked the chain around her waist with. Dammit.

There was no food, but her stomach was in so much turmoil she wasn't worried about food anyway. There'd been so many lean days in the past, days when she'd put off meals so that Lily could have new shoes, or take a trip with her school, that going without food wasn't a big deal to her. She'd learned last summer about some diet thing called intermittent fasting, which was basically what she'd been doing all these years. Even when times had been a little better, she'd often gone without so that she could send Lily a nice outfit, or to help Aunt Katie with the power bills during the cold months.

When she'd learned about the benefits of fasting, she'd decided she was ahead of the times, that's all. Now, she just had to prepare her mind for no food, but a lot of water. Not even broth, just plain old water. She could do this, she knew she could.

An outer door slammed, leaving Roxie to wonder if she'd been left alone, or if someone had come in. There was no new noise outside the room, so she believed she'd been left alone.

The plastic wrapped around the water bottles was a pain in the ass, especially when her hands were tied, but she managed to get one bottle free. Taking the bottle with her, Roxie went to the wall and slid down it to the floor. How had she ended up here?

Her thoughts flew back to that night, to the flames and the pain that had nearly destroyed her when she learned her parents were dead. It had been a relief to find out Aunt Katie was still alive, she'd forgotten for a little while that Aunt Katie had taken that night off, but still. She'd gone into a deep depression that only her pregnancy had been able to relieve.

Her thoughts came forward, spinning through each

success in her career, the awards she'd received, the piles of cash she'd made and spent. Then the fire at Elmo's, the way things had turned out with her ex-boyfriend. The insanity that had taken place over the last few months, over her whole life, hadn't prepared her for sitting in the dark with a bucket for a toilet.

Lincoln's face flashed in her mind. So many impressions of him had imprinted on her brain. The way he sighed and his face relaxed when he slid into her. The way he smiled at her when she ate the pancakes he brought as a treat for her. Then, many different images, from a pleased smile, to relief during their time in Cambodia, their stolen nights there, in her tent. The anger on his face when he'd confronted her about Lily. The coldness as he'd told her he was taking custody of her daughter away.

The uncertainty she thought she'd caught a glimpse of when he'd shown up to confront Nick. That had confused her, but now, she wondered if he'd been unsure about his decisions.

She could only hope that he was already looking for her. That she hadn't burned the bridge with him entirely, and that he hadn't washed his hands of her.

"Please, let Lincoln be looking for me," Roxie said out loud, just to break the silence. And just in case it made it more meaningful to whoever might be listening. "And also, if I die, please don't let my daughter hurt too much.

Don't let her live her life with the pain I've had to endure. And don't let my death be horrific either, please. Not for me, but for her."

Roxie's head fell back to the wall. She was tired, so tired now.

Instead of going to sleep, she reached down in the dark to try to untie the rope around her ankles. She wasn't going to hobble all over the place. If they wanted her feet tied, they'd have to tie them back up. There was also no way she was going to be able to hover over a bucket and pee if her ankles were tied together. It was one thing to squat behind a bush and pee, but using a bucket with your ankles tied was impossible.

Roxie was fairly certain she'd torn one nail loose from the nailbed by the time the rope loosened up and she pulled it off, but she managed it. She shuffled her legs on the floor, trying to get the circulation back into her feet. She had to wiggle her toes and both feet when the blood rushed back in painfully. That was okay, at least her feet were free.

She thought about gnawing at the rope around her wrists with her teeth, but decided to forego that horror for now. There was no way to get the padlock off the chain around her waist. Even if she got her hands free, she'd still be locked to the chain and wall.

But what if she could get the chain loose from the wall? Roxie pushed herself up from the floor and felt around on the wall until she found the bolt the chain was attached to. The chain links were thick, heavy metal, so it was hardly a surprise when the bolt the chain was attached to was much thicker and didn't budge a bit. She yanked at the chain, but the bolt still didn't shift.

A shriek filled the air, an angry sound, not one of fear.

She was afraid she'd die, but the anger was keeping the fear at bay for now.

With a sigh, Roxie slid down the wall, wondering if the room had been prepared just for her, or if someone else had once inhabited the space. There was no doubt in her mind that those men who'd brought her here were killers. There'd been something dead and malicious in stinky-guy's eyes that worried her, a lot. But who had hired them?

There were no answers and, for the first time, she began to wonder if she'd ever get any. Or if they'd just leave her here to die of starvation. If she was careful with the water, dehydration wouldn't get her, but hunger might. If Lincoln didn't find her before it got that far, starvation would definitely kill her.

Dark thoughts fought to replace the anger that kept her from sprawling out and falling asleep. Exhaustion tugged at her, but she fought it off. That must be from shock and maybe whatever they'd injected her with.

Carefully, she brought the bottle up between her legs, undid the cap, and took a long swig of the water.

She wanted to put off having to use that bucket as long as she could, but she was thirsty. Besides, a little pee never hurt anybody. It was the other thing she had to worry about. Although, if she didn't get any food, then she wouldn't have to worry about the fact that there was no toilet paper, would she?

The situation was impossible, but there was nothing else she could do, for now. The only option available was to wait, even if she hated that option. Beggars can't be choosers, that was something Aunt Katie had said often when Roxie was growing up. It was a truth Roxie had faced many times before.

Sighing deeply, Roxie gave in to the exhaustion. She cushioned her head on her hands, wishing the assholes had left her a blanket at least. It was cold and those bastards had taken her coat off. All she had on was the sweater and her jeans. The temperature would drop even further, as the day went on.

The thought chilled Roxie's blood even more than the air outside her body. Was that how they planned to kill her? Let her freeze to death?

6

Lincoln

*L*incoln ran a hand through his brown hair while casting his eyes of a deeper brown around the kitchen of his house. Roxie was nowhere, absolutely nowhere to be found. How could she have slipped past his security people, and every other fucker watching her?

Anger flushed his cheeks and clenched the muscles in his jaw, but he wasn't sure who to direct the anger at. He didn't know for sure whether Roxie had just got pissed off and run away or if someone had taken her. That left him not knowing what to do and he was not a man who enjoyed feeling helpless in any way.

He paced the floor, decided to have some coffee, then decided he didn't need any more caffeine. When you were already pacing, adding more anxiety wasn't a good idea. He stuck his hands in his pockets, glad that Katie was there to get Lily from school. He'd managed to get her off to school without too many fibs about where her mother was.

The truth was, he didn't know where Roxie was. He didn't want to explain that to his daughter, not until he knew something was wrong. If she'd just taken off, that was one thing, but what if something had happened to her?

The muscles around his heart knotted up intensely, making him hiss from the discomfort. Is this how she'd felt when he was missing? Like the world was about to collapse on top of him?

"Don't panic yet, Lincoln. Not yet." His phone chirped and he moved to the table to check the notification. It was from Kai. There was no sign of her anywhere in South Carolina, it said, but there was someone staying with his siblings at the old house. Was it her? Had she gone to New York?

Lincoln scrolled through his phone then hit the call button under June's name. He started to pace again as the call went through. June's voice answered but it was her voicemail.

"Shit!" Lincoln mumbled, flicking the end call button angrily.

June might be doing rounds or performing an operation. She'd call him back when she had time.

Lincoln left the house, sliding the phone into his back pocket as he did so. He walked along the surf, staying far enough out of it to keep his shoes dry. His eyes were on the horizon, off in the distance, tracking the sails of a yacht, but he didn't really see it. His mind was on Roxie.

If she was the guest at the house then she'd decided to go to New York for some reason. Why, he couldn't say, but he knew she'd have her reasons. Perhaps it was something to do with Lily, or maybe not. There'd been no closure for her when her parents died. He hadn't been able to find the answers, though he did have a few leads about those two guys she'd seen. He'd caught brief glimpses of the men that night, but it had been enough to implant their images in his memory.

He had worked with some of the best people in the world to find answers, but there was a piece of the puzzle missing, a very vital piece. Without that piece, he couldn't move forward.

It hadn't helped that Roxie's parents had been intensely private about their families, and had done a lot of work to hide their origins. Lincoln knew people had their reasons for doing things like that, but the things her parents had done to obscure their pasts made it hard for Lincoln to get a grip on what had happened exactly.

She wouldn't find answers up there, she'd find only danger. Someone had deliberately set that fire, had murdered her parents, he was as convinced of it now as he'd been the night they died. Her father had loved her mother deeply, and he'd loved Roxie just as intensely. He'd decided to move the whole family to Paris to keep them together. A man who went to that much trouble didn't kill his wife in a fit of rage and leave his child an orphan.

Something had gone terribly wrong in their lives, and that meant Roxie was now in danger if she was in New York.

Swiping at his face with both hands to clear his mind, Lincoln inhaled deeply and then reached for his phone. He sent a text to both of his PAs, not sure which was in the office today, and directed them to get a plane to New York organized for him, and to have a car ready for him there. He then sent a text to Kai to up the security around his house and to let his friend know where he was going, before he called Katie, who was out shopping again.

"Hi Katie, I'll be gone this evening. No, I don't know when I'll be back. Keep Lily safe for me, okay?" Lincoln paused, listening to her question. "Yes, I'm going to look for Chloe. I'll let you know as soon as I know something, yes."

Lincoln ended the call as he walked into the house

and packed a bag quickly. He had clothes and other things in New York, but he'd need a coat as soon as he landed, and some of his electronics. He was in his car and on the way to the airport when June called him back.

"Hey brother, what's going on?" June asked nonchalantly. That was a clue that she was hiding something. June always came to the point on the phone with him, especially during office hours.

"She's there, isn't she?" Lincoln said, knowing the hands-free mode in the car would pick up his voice.

"Who?" June asked vapidly, and Lincoln's eyes narrowed on the display in the center of the car.

"Don't fuck around with me right now, June. Is Roxie up there?" He waited, tapping his fingers on the steering wheel at a stoplight.

"Dammit, Lincoln. Why do I keep ending up in the middle between you two?" June protested, but her sigh of resignation told him she wasn't going to put up a fight. "She still has her phone off?"

"I guess, it goes straight to voicemail, and she hasn't even looked at the messages I've sent her. So, she's there?" He already had her confirmation by admitting she knew Roxie's phone was off, but he wanted it to be clear.

"She is. I left her at the cemetery with my other phone. You have the number for that one, don't you?

Not that she'll answer it, why would she?" June sighed again, but Lincoln was too busy frowning at the light that was taking too long to turn green to notice.

"What do you mean, you left her at the cemetery? Why would you leave her alone like that?" Lincoln wanted to strangle his sister, who was always too trusting in these situations.

She was a great doctor but in her personal life? Well, she was a bit of a pushover. Normally, her kind and trusting nature would be a good thing, but she'd had a few mishaps over the years because of it. And now she'd left Roxie alone in a cemetery, in New York, the last damn place she should be.

"She was upset, it was the first time she'd been to their grave, you know? I had to get into the office, and she said she'd get a taxi. That's why she has my other phone, so she could call the taxi to pick her up. I'm sure she's fine anyway, Lincoln. She knows how to take care of herself. Stop smothering her." June's timidity gave way to anger as she went on, but Lincoln ignored it. Now wasn't the time for his sister to grow a backbone.

"I'm not smothering her. I'm trying to keep her alive. I'll see you later." Lincoln ended the call just as the light changed. The tires spun a little on the asphalt when he gunned the engine, but he didn't care. If the police wanted to give him a ticket, they'd have to do it from the air. Nobody was stopping him from getting on that plane.

The plane was delayed because of a storm, which did little to ease Lincoln's anger or helplessness. He hated feeling that way, but he'd accepted it, for now. There was nothing he could do bar having someone bring him his car and drive to New York. That would take even longer than the delays were taking, though, so there was no sense in doing that.

He'd had a lot of time to think, sitting and waiting for answers, and he knew he'd been stupid. Yeah, he had a right to be angry about Roxie keeping Lily from him all this time, but that was shit he'd have to deal with. She'd done the best she could in the situation she'd been put in. She hadn't asked for her parents to be killed, to lose her home, or to end up with a baby the first time she'd had sex at eighteen.

He had to give her some credit, actually, for having Lily and keeping her out of the world's lens for so long. He'd had no idea the little girl had existed at all, yet, there she was, full of life, love, and laughter. His daughter.

She was a beautiful girl, and he'd never known he could love someone he barely knew so much, but there he was, sitting in an airport, with misty eyes as he thought about his daughter and her mother. He hadn't wanted a wife, or even a girlfriend, although he had wanted children. His mother had poisoned the well, so to speak, with her serial weddings.

Lincoln had come to wonder if the woman loved the thrill and romance of weddings more than the actual marriage over time, and that had colored his perspective on women and their ability to stay in a relationship. Sure, there were other people he knew who'd been married for decades, but he couldn't shake the idea that he never wanted to get married himself.

Until Roxie came back into his life.

He'd almost bought her an engagement ring when they visited Tiffany's that day. He'd nearly proposed to her then. But, if he had, he'd have regretted it, he could see that now. There had still been secrets between them then. There may be more, but he had a feeling now he knew everything there was to know about Roxie.

He respected her need to have things unplugged around her when she left a house. He knew she hated goat's cheese but loved every other variety of cheese out there. He knew she'd tried her best to raise her daughter without bringing shame or dishonor to the girl. He also knew she loved deeply and wholeheartedly when it mattered.

He'd seen her with her friends, with his friends, how she treated everyone with respect, right down to the waitstaff in restaurants. And when he'd seen her with Lily? He'd suspected she may never love anyone as much as she loved their daughter. Which was fine, because a child deserved all of its parent's love.

Which was another reason he knew she hadn't run away from Lily. She'd gone to New York looking for answers to the questions that plagued her in the dark hours, in the quiet moments at work, when she had time to think the thoughts that made her eyes go dark with sadness.

But there were people in New York who were probably still looking for her. A group of people that would stop at nothing to destroy her. Why, he had no clue, but that group of people was ruthless, cruel, and more dangerous than any other opponent Lincoln had ever had to deal with. He wasn't afraid of them, but he also wasn't stupid. He knew taking them on, confronting them, wasn't the way to go. He'd only get his head blown off, without a blink of an eye.

No, he'd have to do this with caution, if they hadn't taken her already. And if they had, well, he'd do whatever it took to get her back.

The plane was delayed another fifteen minutes and Lincoln finally couldn't stand it anymore. He paced the floor as he called June yet again.

"Hello?" She said when she answered the call.

"Have you found her yet?" He demanded, not having the patience for polite greetings.

"No, Lincoln. I had rounds, then an emergency with

a new patient. I'm not sure why you're so freaked out. I'm sure she's fine."

"Are you done for the day now?" Lincoln had crammed his fingertips into the spot over the bridge of his nose, trying to ease the headache pounding to life behind his eyes.

"Yes, but I still don't know what has you so worked up." June was probably rolling her eyes. Lincoln could almost hear it over the phone, she sounded so impatient, but he didn't give a fuck what she thought.

"I don't have time for this right now. I need you to go and find her. Take her to your apartment. Don't let her leave until I get there, understand me?" He paused, waiting for her answer.

"I guess. Damn, big brother, you could ask nicely, you know?" June spoke testily, her own ire rising.

Good, she might take him seriously now. "I could, sure. But you'd still be sitting on your ass, twiddling your thumbs if I didn't light a fire under it. Now get out there and find Roxie. I'm getting on a plane." Lincoln had heard the boarding call while he spoke to his sister and wasn't about to cause another delay. He grabbed his suitcase and started to walk quickly to the line.

"See you soon then. Safe journey," June said without any sarcasm at all. She'd already forgiven him.

"See you soon. Go find Roxie." He hung up the phone and handed over his boarding pass to the agent with her hand out. She scanned the pass and wished Lincoln a pleasant journey. He smiled back, but it didn't reach his eyes.

The flight soon took off without a hitch. Lincoln worked on a few items in his email that couldn't wait before he settled into his seat and tried to relax. His thoughts spun around in his head though, making it hard to do anything except tap his fingertips against the hard plastic of the chair he occupied.

"Drink, sir?" A male voice asked, and Lincoln looked up to see the flight attendant with a cart in front of him.

"Scotch, please," Lincoln said, watching as it was poured. "Thanks."

"Anything else?" The blond man asked with a smile that was pleasant, if not quite real.

"I'll take a coffee, too, thanks." Lincoln took the coffee, packets of sugar, and small tub of creamer the man gave him. He wasn't really interested in the coffee, but he didn't want to drink the scotch on its own. He'd need to wash it down with something.

The plane would land soon, and he'd need to be on his toes from that moment on. Instinct told him that something was wrong. He'd learned to trust that instinct a long time ago.

7

Lincoln

"Thanks for arranging this meeting," Lincoln said to Paulo, a friend of his with connections to the less than savory parts of New York City life. Lincoln didn't get his fingers dirty if he could help it, so Paulo was an asset at times like these.

"It's my pleasure, Lincoln. Just don't make me regret it," the older man with salt-and-pepper hair and a finely-lined face said. His hard gaze met Lincoln's across the car Lincoln was driving, a warning from brown eyes much darker than Lincoln's. "I have to live here. Don't forget that."

"I'll do my best," Lincoln said, in lieu of a promise. He wasn't going to promise a damned thing to anybody when it came to finding out where Roxie was. He'd move mountains and destroy whoever he had to if it meant he'd get her back. If that included stepping on a few toes as well, so be it. He'd crush anything that stood in his way.

His plane had landed without word from June, or anyone else for that matter. He'd decided not to call June back, he didn't want to panic her more than he had. Instead, he'd called Paulo, intending to get some answers. If June hadn't heard from Roxie, something was wrong. No amount of reassurance from June or anyone else would make him believe he was wrong. Something wasn't right, he could feel it, he *knew* it.

The car pulled into an open bay of a warehouse and came to a stop. *Why were these meetings always in fucking cold, damp warehouses?* Lincoln thought to himself, looking out of the window of the car. He could see the typical chains hanging creepily down from the ceiling, and the way the floor gleamed with water, taking it all in without a verbal comment. If the guy he was about to meet wanted to be the typical mobster without a clue, he'd keep his judgments to himself. So long as he got answers, he didn't care if the guy wanted to meet in the Statue of Liberty with Lincoln holding a dozen roses.

"That's them," Paulo said and opened his door when another car pulled in from the other side of the warehouse. Lincoln followed him out, pulling his black wool coat around him and buttoning it up. He stuck his hands in his pockets, feeling for the small 9mm pistol he'd tucked into the deep left side. The gun had been left in a small box on the backseat of the car he'd had his PA arrange for him.

He'd removed the gun from the box, placed it in the pocket, and put the coat on before going to pick up Paulo. The older man, slightly portly after a car accident left him with a broken leg that had never quite healed right, hadn't suspected that Lincoln had the gun, or if he had, he hadn't said anything about it. It wouldn't matter if he had, Lincoln wasn't going into this meeting unarmed or unprepared.

There may be no need for the gun in the end, but better safe than sorry.

"Let me do the talking," Paulo said, waving Lincoln back a little to stand behind him.

Lincoln took up the position, but wasn't about to stand there like a spare dick if Paulo couldn't get the answers Lincoln wanted. His friendship with the man had begun a few years back when Lincoln first started his fintech venture. Paulo had invested in the startup and had made a tidy profit from the venture. Lincoln didn't ask where Paulo's money came from, and Paulo had offered his services if Lincoln ever needed them. Up to now, Lincoln had not needed those services.

Lincoln would do his best to stay calm and collected, but if this mob guy didn't give him some answers,

Lincoln would gladly break his neck. Which would get him nowhere but with a contract on his head, put out by the guy's family. Even he knew not to mess with the fucking mafia, and the guy in the back of that black Maserati was definitely in the mob. Now if he could just remember that and not curb-stomp the guy, that would be good, Lincoln reminded himself silently.

The mob guy's name was Matteo Mazza, now head of the Alfonsi family. He was no relation to the Alfonsis but he was related to the old boss of the family, a woman, oddly enough. She'd taken over the organization when her husband was taken out quite a few years ago. It seemed she'd appointed this Matteo guy as her successor when she decided to retire from mob life. Nobody knew where the woman was, but Matteo hadn't been hard to find. He wasn't often in this part of the world anymore, but he was now.

That was another reason Lincoln suspected Matteo was behind Roxie's disappearance. The guy was in town just when Roxie went silent. That seemed too convenient, and Lincoln couldn't ignore it. Suspecting the guy was a reach, if you didn't know that the two men who had been at Roxie's the night her parents died worked for Matteo. Lincoln also suspected they might be the men Roxie's ex, Nathan, had been in debt to. Or the family that shithead owed money to, at least. That was two too many connections, so Lincoln was meeting with

Matteo to find out what the fucking problem was and to get Roxie back.

"Paulo, good to see you." A man around Lincoln's age stepped up to the older man with his hand held out. He was in a tailored, camel-color overcoat with a black scarf around his neck. His black hair was cut stylishly, and his skin was tanned. And that wasn't the kind of tan you got from a sunbed, it was from somewhere tropical with lots of sunlight.

"Good to see you too, kid. How's the wife?" Paulo asked, taking Matteo's hand. Paulo wore an overcoat as well, but his was tight around his stomach. Lincoln looked at the back of Paulo's coat, noting the threads in the back seam were pulled tight. Paulo needed a new coat, or to lose some weight.

This was all just a way for Lincoln to distract himself while Paulo talked to the mafia guy, but Lincoln still caught the gist of the conversation. They must be on good terms if Paulo could call him kid, Lincoln decided, and let the gun in his hand go, for now.

"She's good, Paulo. Suffering a little, but that's to be expected." Matteo shrugged a little, his gaze shifting to Lincoln. "Who's this?"

"This is Lincoln Young. He needs some information, if you can help him out, Matteo." Paulo gestured for Lincoln to move forward. Lincoln walked up, his hand out, even though he wanted to punch the guy with the defined jawline that he'd probably break his fist on.

Hard gray eyes looked Lincoln over, as if summing him up with one look. Matteo seemed to come to some kind of decision when his eyes met Lincoln's as he nodded in approval. "What can I do for you, Mr. Young?"

"I need to know where Roxie is," Lincoln answered shortly, not letting Paulo direct the conversation. It might be a breech in protocol, but Lincoln didn't exactly give a fuck. At all.

"Who?" Matteo inquired calmly, his eyes softly blinking once before he gazed back at Lincoln steadily.

"Roxie Simpson. Your guys have her, right? I want her back. Name your price, it's yours." Lincoln stood his ground, not backing down, even when two men stepped out of the car, guns on display in their hands.

The two giants with black hair, twins by the looks of it, moved behind Lincoln, their arms crossed casually, but the guns still there. All they'd have to do was lift their hands and they could take Lincoln down before he even blinked, and he knew it. Best to try to negotiate, for the moment.

"I really don't know who you're talking about," Matteo responded, waving the men back. He wasn't threatened by Lincoln, but that wasn't a smart move. All

Lincoln had to do was lift his own hand, still in his pocket, and the man would be dead at his feet.

This was no time for a pissing contest though.

"Bullshit," Lincoln spit out, ready to pull out his phone and show him the photos of the men that had been there the night Roxie's parents died. They were older, but still the same men. And they were with Matteo in the pictures.

"Excuse me? Do you know who I am?" Matteo asked quietly, his eyes barely changing, but there was now a deadly tilt to them, a threat in the tightness at the corners.

"Yes, I know who you fucking are, I just don't care. Roxie is missing, and I know your guys had something to do with it." Lincoln paused, gathering his composure, or trying to. "What's your price?"

"Look, I have a wife I care a great deal for. I'd do anything to get her back if she was missing, so I'll let the disrespect go, but I'm serious. I have no reason to lie to you. I don't know where this Roxie person is." Matteo held out empty hands, his eyes now calm and, from what Lincoln could detect, honest. "If I had some problem with a woman, I'd never kidnap her, anyway. Especially one I don't know. Besides, do I look like I'm short of money?"

Lincoln took a deep breath, his eyes catching the glare Paulo sent his way. He was pissing Matteo off and that wouldn't help him. Lincoln wasn't sure why he'd trust a guy in the mafia but he could feel it, this guy was telling him the truth. He had no idea where Roxie was. But those guys did, they had to be in on this somewhere. "Listen, I don't mean any offense, I just want to get her back. Can I show you something on my phone?"

Lincoln held his hands up in the air now, trying to show he meant no harm. The gigantic twins took a menacing step forward, but Matteo waved them back. "Please. If it helps explain why you brought this to me, I'd appreciate seeing it."

Matteo's voice had a strange sound to it, like he wanted to say something else, but he was holding back. Lincoln had a feeling there was more going on here than he'd been able to figure out so far. Taking his phone out of an inside pocket of his coat, Lincoln scrolled through it to find the images of the men with Matteo. "These guys? You know them, right?"

One of the giants came up to get the phone from Lincoln and carried it back to Matteo. Lincoln saw the moment Matteo recognized the guys and his own image. "Obviously, I do."

"Right, that means you know Roxie then. She's the mother of my daughter, and I want her back."

"I'm sorry, connect the dots for me? What aren't you telling me?" Matteo looked back up at Lincoln, gesturing for the giant to give Lincoln his phone back.

Lincoln put the phone back in his coat and tried to figure out how to verbalize all of this. "They were sent to Roxie's parents' place ten years ago. Their visit saw her dad getting beat up. The second time she saw them, her house was on fire and those two were milling around, throwing the cops off the trail. I've been investigating this for a long time now. Those guys are connected to that fire. They're connected to your… organization. They're somehow connected to Roxie disappearing now."

"I see," Matteo said, that jawline of his hardening as his eyes turned inward.

Lincoln waited while the man had a little think about this new info. It was easy to connect the dots, once you knew the dots connected. There was still the missing question of why, but Lincoln could only assume Roxie's parents owed those guys money. That was the only connection he'd been able to come up with. Nothing else existed to show a connection between Roxie's family and the Alfonsi family. It might have been a personal matter between one of those guys and Roxie's parents, but Lincoln knew enough about these mob families to know that the individuals rarely did anything on their own, not without consequences for potentially drawing heat to the family.

"I may have some information about this matter,

after all. Excuse me a moment, please?" Matteo asked but walked away before Lincoln agreed.

I guess when you have that much power you don't wait for someone's approval, Lincoln thought to himself. He looked over at Paulo, who nodded in support. Lincoln gave a curt nod of his own and leaned back against the hood of the car he'd driven to the warehouse. He slid his hands down into his pockets, giving off the air of relaxed patience. Even if he wanted to jump up and down on Matteo's head until he spilled all the information he may or may not have.

"Stay calm, my friend," Paulo said as he came up next to Lincoln and took up the same pose. Calm, relaxed patience.

Lincoln breathed in, nodded again, and tried to wait without blowing up. His phone buzzed and he reached into his pocket to get it. A message from June.

"I can't find Roxie. What's going on Lincoln? WTH?"

Lincoln frowned down at his phone, knowing that WTH meant what the hell. Finally, June had caught on. Something was up and time was wasting away. The longer Roxie was missing, the more likely it was they wouldn't find her. That's why he stood there and waited for Matteo to climb back out of that masterpiece of a car and get back to him. If he had any information, Lincoln would need it.

A long twenty minutes passed before Matteo

climbed out of the car, his face grim as his eyes met Lincoln's. "I can't tell you where or why, but I can tell you I think I know who is behind all of this."

Lincoln stared at the man, silently urging him to go on.

"If I'm right, this Roxie person is in a lot of danger. I'll offer any help I can give you. But you have to promise me one thing. If you get any information about this person, you have to share it with me. I'm going to nail them to the wall and flay them alive." Matteo's eyes were bright with the scent of revenge. Lincoln knew that much without asking, it was clear on the man's face. Whoever had Roxie was on Matteo's hit list. Fucking great.

8

Roxie

*R*oxie was cold. Shivering so badly she couldn't stop it cold. The kind of cold that could kill. She turned to the wall, hoping her body would reflect heat off the wall and back into her body, but the cold wall just seemed to absorb what little heat she put off. Fear of dying was front and center in her mind.

"Get up, move around, get your blood circulating, girl," Roxie said to herself, and stood up in the dark room. She wouldn't knock anything over but the bucket, she'd learned that from her earlier search of the room, so she began to pace, walking as fast as she could back and forth, at the very end of the thick chain.

She walked, and walked, and then walked some

more, despite how tired she was. Every time she stopped walking, she felt the cold air on her face and started to move again. Her worry was what would happen when she stopped. She'd built up a fine sheen of sweat on her skin, which was probably enough to make her even colder when she stopped.

And there would come a point when she'd have to stop. She couldn't walk in the small room forever. Her legs would give out, even if she tried to stay on her feet. There was a possibility that Lincoln would be looking for her, but it wasn't certain. Maybe he'd assumed she'd disappeared on him again, like she had all those years ago? He'd taken over the care of their daughter, she had no other real ties, it would be perfectly sane for him to think she'd suddenly decided to leave it all behind and start a new life. Again.

But, June would know something was wrong, right? Roxie had told her she'd talk with her later. And Dr. Bennet would know too. He'd planned to meet with Roxie at some point that day. When Roxie didn't show, there'd be two people who knew that something wasn't right. Wouldn't there?

She could only hope someone would catch on to the fact that she was missing, and wish she'd worn an entire snowsuit out that morning. She'd give anything to have some of those little sachets that heated up, tucked into her coat pockets to keep her freezing fingers warm. They were probably horrible for the environment, but she'd love to have an entire box of them right now and some tape to plaster them over every inch of her skin.

Roxie slapped her hands against her arms, trying to get the blood flowing in them again. The cold was getting worse, but there was nothing she could do to help herself. Those two assholes had left her here to die, she knew that now. They weren't coming back for her and this would be the place where she died. Every time she got the urge to sit down, Roxie reminded herself of that.

Once you sit down, you die.

She tried to remember warm days on the beach, hot nights with Lincoln in Cambodia, not for the steamy parts, but for the sweaty, burning heat she'd felt. Maybe if she remembered how hot she'd been, she'd warm up a little bit. Blood rushed to her cheeks, but little else happened.

"Come on, Rox, keep moving." She got on her own case, there was nobody else to do it for her. That had often been the case in her life, though. She'd had to take care of her own problems for so long, it was kind of hard to remember a time when she didn't have to be the grownup. Sure, her parents had taken care of stuff for her before they died, but she'd lived enough for three lifetimes since that day.

Now she was in the deepest shit of her life, and she was once again alone.

Roxie stopped pacing, staring around the dark room, straining to penetrate the darkness with eyes that weren't up to the job. She needed night vision, but that wasn't something most humans were born with. Taking a deep breath, she walked back to the bolt in the wall. She'd tried to loosen it up dozens of times, but nothing made the bolt budge. There was no way she'd manage to get it out of the wall, even when she'd tried to use the chain as a lever, the stupid thing hadn't moved.

"Fuck me," Roxie moaned, going back to her march.

She'd tried to figure out if there was a way to release the padlock that held the chain together at her waist, but there was nothing she could push into the lock. She'd tried to push the chain down her hips, or over her boobs, but she'd only managed to bruise herself doing that. Still, a few bruises or a broken bone here and there might be worth it, if they got her out of the chain and out of that room.

She'd already felt around in her pockets, only to realize the men must have removed the phone June gave her. She was lucky they'd left her with her clothes and her coat, men with eyes that dead could have done far worse to her. That wasn't worth thinking about, she reminded herself, and went back to pacing.

Her legs finally started to cramp after an hour of

pacing, or what felt like an hour, and Roxie dropped to the floor in agony. Her left leg was cramping so bad she was almost screaming in agony. She pointed her toes back at her chest, a trick she'd learned from another dancer long ago, shrieking as the pain increased, but then it started to fade away. A dull ache remained in her calf, a pain that wouldn't go, no matter how much she stretched the leg.

She'd had to deal with cramps very often when she first started dancing as a child. She hadn't learned the toe trick until she became a stripper. Back then, she'd been getting a lot of leg cramps, probably from dehydration, but on the advice of the same dancer, she'd started to eat a banana every day, for the potassium. It was time to start eating bananas again, something she'd forgotten about in all of the turmoil lately.

She hadn't expected the past year to go quite as it had. Well, things had initially gone south when Elmo's burned down. There'd been enough good things in her life, at that point, to make up for the bad that came along after, but the good things had slowly petered out. Lincoln came back into her life, which had seemed bad, then good, then the most wonderful thing to happen to her. He'd been kidnapped by her dickhead ex-boyfriend, which had been one of the lowest points of her life, but they'd managed to get through that with Lincoln coming out alive.

Now she was the one in harm's way. But had she ever really not been in danger? Between Nathan and the boogeymen from her past, it felt like she'd always had a cloud hanging over her head. Nathan had brought more danger into her life when he'd become involved with some kind of gangsters he owed money to, then he'd developed a drug problem. She'd needed that like she needed a hole in the head.

And the men from that night? The night her parents died.

Was that what this was about? She'd known there was some kind of danger in coming back to New York, to this part of New York, at least. There'd never been any answers, was that because the danger hadn't ended when her parents died?

If they thought she knew something besides who the men were–well, she didn't know their names, but she knew their faces–they were mistaken. There was no way she could identify them, unless the cops showed her pictures and asked if this was the men she'd seen beating up her father, and at the property the night of the fire. So was there really any need for all of this?

Unless this was some new threat, she decided, folding her arms around her chest to try to hold in her body heat. Could this be something to do with Lincoln and his business? Was there some enemy out there who wanted to get back at him, make him try to give up on something he was doing?

No, she'd been kidnapped in her old hometown. This had to have something to do with her old life, her old name. Which only strengthened her stance that her parents were murdered, despite what the police around here wanted her to believe. Were those police in on it perhaps? It wasn't a new idea, it was one she'd circled around before, but she didn't want to think they were dirty cops. She could handle inept policemen, but bad cops?

Lily's face popped into her mind and Roxie sighed with a sniffle. Tears wouldn't help anything, but Roxie's baby girl might be what got her through this. Lily was conceived the night Roxie's parents died, that was reason enough to keep her, to give birth to her. From the very first ultrasound picture, Roxie had loved her daughter.

She'd had to live like she didn't have a child and that had hurt her a lot over the years, but she'd done what she thought was best for her daughter. Roxie's life hadn't been easy, even when she was flush with cash. Living with Aunt Katie had given Lily some stability, a kind of safety that Roxie couldn't provide her with.

Roxie remembered the day Lily was born like it had only been hours ago. Lily's face had been smooshed up, and she'd had a shock of black hair that made Roxie giggle. Aunt Katie had been there, helping Roxie to change the baby, showing her how to hold her and feed her. Everything Roxie had needed to know or needed to have done, Aunt Katie had been there for her. And the first picture taken of Roxie and Lily together had been taken by that same woman.

Those two people were all the family she had, and she'd do her best to stay alive for them.

Roxie pushed herself back up the wall and started to walk again.

As she paced the same route out across the room, Roxie remembered the day she left New York, headed for a new life. Aunt Katie had taken Lily from her with the promise that she would keep her safe, no matter what. Roxie knew that promise still stood. If the worst should happen here, Aunt Katie would continue to be there for Lily.

Small comfort, right now, but then there was Lincoln too. Lily would have those two to help her to grow up, to be the woman she should be. They would keep her from the kind of life Roxie had to live. They would make sure little Lily didn't have to fend for herself, they would make sure Lily could be whatever she wanted to be.

What if she wanted to be a pole dancer? The thought cropped up suddenly, making Roxie smile. Lincoln would probably have a few choice words about that, but Aunt Katie? She'd tell Lily to follow her heart. She hadn't judged Roxie when Roxie finally told her how she was making money. She'd just said she knew Roxie had to do what she had to do.

Lily had been so worried about meeting her dad, but he'd been so ready to meet her. Which reminded Roxie that there were still things she hadn't told Lincoln. In a way, she was making the same mistake she'd made all those years ago. She'd run away to find answers this time though. That was the difference. She'd planned to go back when she had those answers. She'd planned to tell him everything, once she knew what had happened in the past. Well, she hadn't actually got that far, but she had a vague plan to go back to Myrtle Beach. To claim her daughter back from the man who seemed to want to take over her completely. To tell him everything he needed to know.

Her hand went to her stomach, hunger gnawing away in there. She'd eaten plenty that morning, but it must be after five now. That meant she'd missed lunch, not something unusual for her. Still, she was hungry, but hopefully, it was just boredom more than actual hunger. Her hand remained at her stomach, cradling her fingers under her sweater for warmth.

Yes, there was at least one more secret to tell Lincoln. If she got the chance, that is.

Roxie went back to the wall and let her body slide down gently. She did some stretching this time, trying to keep another cramp at bay. It wasn't easy with the chain around her waist, but she did manage to do a few stretches that should help.

When she'd completed what she could, she sat down on the cold floor. She was too tired to get up for more walking but she'd done a few dances, with a chain around her waist, which hadn't been many, but even that was too much to think about right now. Sitting down could be a death sentence, but she needed to rest.

"Just a few minutes, then I'll get back up," she sighed out, even though there wasn't anyone to hear her. "Why does it have to be winter?"

Of course, there was no answer, but she hadn't expected one.

"What else can I do?" She wondered aloud, tucking her hands in her armpits, beneath her clothes. She tilted her head forward so her hair fell around her face like a curtain. She'd let it down earlier, when her ears got cold, now, she was trying to warm up her entire face. "It's like a freezer in here. Shit."

A tingle in her bladder made her get up again. If she sweated all of the water out of her body, she wouldn't have to pee, right? That's what she hoped anyway, as she walked quickly, trying to build up a sweat. She did not want to use that stupid bucket if she could help it. Who knew if it was even clean? Which, she knew, wouldn't matter if her bladder became insistent, but still, it was gross to think about.

She finally admitted defeat when her bladder ached deeper, despite the slight sweat she'd built up with a good dose of walking fast. "I don't need to add dehydration to hypothermia."

She did what she had to do, not caring if she hit the bucket or not at this point, almost hoping she didn't at the same time. Not because it meant someone else would have to clean it up but because she really didn't want to be anywhere near that awful thing.

That's when she heard a noise outside the room. A noise that sounded like people coming in. Was it rescuers or her kidnappers? Her pulse began to pound as she stared in the general direction of the door, waiting to see if this was over with, or just the beginning. Or maybe the end of it all.

9

Roxie

"I see you've used the facilities. Well done," a woman said in a slight accent, in her late fifties or early sixties, as she walked into the room, flicking on a light as she did so.

Roxie stared at her from the floor, her lips sealed in shock. A woman was behind this?

The woman was of Italian descent, with black hair, dark brown eyes, and the olive skin that bespoke her heritage. She was a thin woman with an expensive Dior dress on her slim frame, surrounded almost completely with a thick fur coat. Roxie decided the woman could be older now that she was standing under the light, plastic surgery may have hidden a year or two.

"Do I meet your expectations?" The woman asked

with a laugh that revealed perfectly straight, gleaming white teeth. "I suppose I don't. If I had to guess, I'd say you were expecting a man. That happens a lot, quite a lot."

The woman's words trailed off as she came closer to look at Roxie. "You look just like your mother, do you know that?"

"You knew my mother?" Roxie asked, surprised at this. She blinked in confusion, her blue eyes on the woman who moved almost like a snake, a very deadly snake. The woman's eyes locked onto Roxie, and if a tiny black tongue had darted out of her thin face, it wouldn't have surprised Roxie one bit.

"I did, briefly, yes. She wasn't very interesting, and she had no idea who I was at the time, but no matter." The woman's hands, encased in black leather gloves, waved slightly as she looked around the room. "Clarence, can you bring a chair in for me, please?"

The man with the extremely scary eyes came in, a kitchen chair in his hands. His eyes were as dead as they always were, but even his lips were turned down now, in a frown or a smirk, Roxie couldn't tell which. That made him scarier, whichever expression it was. That was the face of a killer. And she watched serial killer documentaries, she'd seen a few killers.

"Aren't you even a little afraid?" The woman interrupted Roxie as she kept track of the stinky guy. He still smelled of unwashed body and far too much cheap cologne, Roxie found out when he put the chair just out of her reach but close enough for her to smell him. Only, the cologne seemed to be even stronger now. Had he put more on because it was later in the day or because he was meeting the woman who must be his boss?

Roxie couldn't imagine there were many women who could order the big guy around like that, so this strange woman must be his boss. Then Roxie remembered the woman had asked a question. "That depends. Did you have something to do with my mother's death?"

Roxie looked the woman in the eye, hoping her face was blank because, of course, she was scared shitless, but she didn't want this woman to know that. This woman looked like she ate fear for breakfast, lunch, and dinner. Letting her know Roxie was afraid would only feed that slithering snake that lived inside of her. Roxie didn't want to do that, so she put on a brave front.

The woman smiled as if reading Roxie's mind, even nodding when Roxie lifted her chin in defiance. "I see. You've decided to be brave. You'll need that bravery later. For now, let's talk."

"About what?" Roxie asked, worrying now that the woman could read her thoughts. Or maybe she was just good at reading expressions, people, Roxie hoped.

"About your parents, my dear. After all, it was your father who started all of this, you see?" The woman held her hands out, indicating the room and Roxie. "If it weren't for him, you wouldn't be here and I would be, well, somewhere, someone else."

"I don't understand," Roxie sputtered, not sure how to answer such a confusing statement. "If my dad had something to do with your circumstances in life, that's not my fault. And, I have to say, you don't seem like you're in such a bad place, right now, compared to me."

"Ah," the woman said with a faint laugh, "a comedienne, are we?"

"No, I'm just stating the obvious." Roxie looked at the woman doubtfully, wondering if antagonizing her was a good idea, but she instinctively fell back on her skills as an exotic dancer, the skills she'd developed over the years dealing with handymen who thought she owed them a blow job or quick fuck in the back of the club because they'd given her a four-dollar tip. Defusing their anger with contempt worked with most of them. They'd stalk off in a huff to try it on the next dancer who came their way.

"I see. Practical, then. I like that. Do you know you were supposed to die that night too? Unfortunately, you slipped out without my guys catching it. That's made things messy for a decade. We've found you a couple of times, but you always slipped away. Until now. You came right to us this time, a gift on a silver platter." The woman smiled a very pleased smile, and Roxie wondered if she'd misjudged her. She might be crazier than Roxie thought to begin with.

She definitely wasn't a well-balanced woman, or a long-lost great-aunt looking to give Roxie an inheritance and a royal title. "Happy to have been of service to you. Can I go now?"

"May I," the woman said, correcting Roxie as though it was a habit she'd developed on someone else. "And no, you may not. And if you try, Clarence there will shoot you in the ankle. You won't be running anywhere after that. But maybe I should make it a knee. If, by some miracle, you make it out of this alive, it would be nice to know you'll never dance again. That should break your spirit. In fact, I may have him do it anyway. Clarence, do you have your gun?"

Roxie shied away, tucking her legs up under her as far as she could, while Clarence waved his gun around before shoving it in the back of his jeans. If she made it out of this alive, the woman had said. If by some miracle, even. Fuck. She was in deep shit.

"Yes, maybe I'll do it anyway. I'll think about it and decide later. You see, your dad fucked my life up a long time ago and I'd really like to repay him. Well, to carry out the rest of his sentence on you."

"But why me? What did I do to you? For that matter, what did he do?" Roxie demanded, but the woman just shook her head, her hair not moving from the French twist it was pinned into tightly.

"I'm not letting you rush me, honey. I've waited ten years for this moment. And lately, well, I've had a few disappointments. Far too many." The woman's eyes became distant, and Roxie could only assume she was thinking over those events. Roxie didn't care if the woman had lived an entire life of disappointments, none of that had anything to do with her. "I'm going to enjoy every single moment that I have with you. I've waited decades, really, to get full revenge. And while I can't totally get that with you, I can get a good deal of satisfaction out of what is about to transpire."

"What is about to transpire?" Roxie asked, but apparently, Clarence had just about had enough of Roxie's questions. He stalked over to Roxie, slapped her so hard her split lip began to bleed again, and walked far enough away that she could breathe again, out of the cloud of stink he gave off.

"Please stop interrupting me, it's rude," Madam in her fur coat said, rolling her eyes. "Did your parents teach you nothing?"

"Well, I lost them when I was eighteen, apparently at your bidding." Roxie couldn't hold the words back and expected the blow that made her ears ring. That still didn't help the ringing or the pain that came with it.

"Yes, it was my bidding. Your father did a very nasty thing to me. An unforgivable thing."

"My father is dead, whatever he did, he's more than paid for." Roxie tried to avoid Clarence's meaty fist and only got clipped on the chin this time. Score one for her!

"No, he didn't pay enough, as far as I'm concerned." The woman's jaw went tight, her lips pursed, and her eyes narrowed as she glared at Roxie. "Bring in the table, Clarence."

Clarence walked out and Roxie waited, wondering if the woman wanted dinner. She expected the big man to bring in a kitchen table that went with the chair. Instead, he brought in what looked like a massage table, but this one came with places in which to tie restraints. Roxie looked at the man, then the woman, a new fear blooming into life. She knew what that table was used for, she'd had something similar installed at Lincoln's house. But this table wouldn't be for pleasurable torture. It would be actual torture. "I'm pregnant."

"And I don't care," the woman said with a pleasant smile, as if she were reacting to the news that Roxie was allergic to peanuts and nothing more. "It will only increase my revenge, killing his grandchild, if you're really pregnant. You could be lying for all I know."

"No, it's true," Roxie answered, but the statement was soft, barely spoken, because she knew it didn't matter.

"Which reminds me, you have another child, don't

you? I can't find a lot about her, but I'll track her down later. I have all the time in the world, now that I'm retired. I'll wipe out your father's entire bloodline, and hers too."

"My mother's?" Roxie was confused, what had her parents done?

"No, not your mother, you silly girl. Put her on the table, Clarence. Leave the chain on for now." The woman waved at the table and Roxie began to fight, glad that she'd managed to get her hands free. She punched the guy in his mouth, felt his nose break with another punch, and gave him a thump in the eye that should cause a fairly decent bruise, but all he did was grunt as though a fly were bothering him. He didn't flinch, he didn't drop her, he just picked her up, dropped her on the table, and proceeded to lock her wrists far too tightly in the handcuffs. He then moved on to her ankles and locked them in as well.

Roxie yanked at the cuffs, even though she knew there was no getting out of them. She'd used, and been in, more than enough to know that. *Fuck.*

She'd played her only hand, and lost. If this woman didn't care that she was pregnant, there was no telling what she'd do now that she had Roxie on this table.

Roxie had known she was pregnant for a while now. She just hadn't wanted to admit it. First, because she was old enough to know how to prevent it, but had messed up anyway. And second, so much shit had been happening that she'd worried she wouldn't be able to carry the baby. Stress was bad for all women, but pregnant women had a hard time dealing with it. There'd been more than one instance when she thought the stress would do her in, but so far, she hadn't died and the tiny little baby inside of her was still growing.

Roxie swallowed hard as the woman came back into her line of sight, a mean smile on her face. She brought a hand up to Roxie's face, tracing the outline of her jaw with a long, scarlet nail. The nail was very sharp, very pointy. Dangerous, Roxie found out, when the woman pushed the tip of the nail on her index finger into the bottom of Roxie's eye socket.

"I could take out both of your eyes, blind you, make sure you can never dance again in that way too. Oh yes, I know all about your life as a dancer." The woman laughed a mirthless laugh, while Roxie tried to pull her eye away from the woman's reach. "Blind dancers aren't much sought after, are they?"

Roxie shook her head no, fear closing her throat. No amount of bravado would stop this crazy bitch, so there was no need to put on a front.

"I could, but I won't. Not right now, anyway. I may change my mind later. We'll see." The woman inhaled deeply before she went to her chair and sat back down again.

That was good. Sitting was good. So long as she was over there, she wasn't here, hurting Roxie or her baby.

"I'm surprised you came back. Especially if you're really pregnant. Why would you put your child in danger like that?" The woman paused, allowing time for Roxie to explain. "Nothing to say? No matter. We can begin then."

"No, don't!" Roxie called out, fighting against the cuffs. "I came back for answers. To find out what happened to my parents. I saw those men beating my dad up, saw them the night of the fire, and wanted to know why they were there. I never believed my dad killed my mother, then himself."

"Oh, very good!" The woman even clapped, but Roxie closed her eyes, thankful for a few minutes of not being tortured. "And that's why you hid for so long. I had a feeling you were suspicious."

"I was. I'd seen them, as I said, and it all just seemed too convenient. My dad had a lot of money, why would he borrow money? Why would he kill my mother and then himself? It didn't make any sense, and I knew something was wrong." Roxie paused to take a deep breath. What else could she say to stall a little longer? "When I had my daughter I knew I had to keep her safe, away from whoever wanted my parents dead. I ran away, hid her when she came along, and…"

Roxie cut her words off, something the woman said

earlier finally dawning on her. "You can't get to my daughter. Her father has her now. You won't get anywhere near her. He'll kill you before you or any of these assholes get near her."

"That may be, but I'll have to try. That's just how it has to be." The woman smirked, but then went on. "Do you remember your Aunt Ruby?"

"Who? I don't have an Aunt Ruby," Roxie frowned, wondering which way this woman was taking her now. Further into crazy-land obviously.

"Pity. She's the reason you're here, as it turns out. With your father's help, she ruined my life. That's why I have you. That slut ruined everything." The woman stood, came close to Roxie, and grabbed her jaw in a painful grip. Roxie stared up at the woman with the insane eyes, worried that her time was nearly done.

10

Lincoln

"**K**ai, I need visual confirmation on this please." Lincoln sent a deed over to his friend's email, wondering who was giggling in the background with Kai. Some woman who would probably go unnamed, if Lincoln knew anything about the man, and he knew quite a few things about Kai. Lincoln frowned at the phone, even if Kai couldn't see the look.

"Right away, Lincoln. I'll have the address checked out by my team." Kai answered, after shushing whoever was with him. "I'll be on the ground in an hour, my friend. Don't worry, we'll get your girl back."

Kai was on his way back to New York on a plane, coming back from a quick trip up to Montreal with a 'friend'. Mmhmm. A friend. Sure. Millions wouldn't believe Kai, but Lincoln did.

Not.

His mind immediately moved back to Roxie after that last thought, and he started digging through the deeds that Matteo had provided him with. He was looking for a building where this mysterious person that Matteo wouldn't name yet might have Roxie. So far, Lincoln and his team on the ground, along with some help from Matteo, had searched a dozen buildings. The hours were ticking by, hours that Lincoln didn't want to waste.

Lincoln had called Kai immediately after Matteo admitted there might be someone after Roxie, even if he hadn't told him the person's name or why she might be after Roxie. Lincoln knew it must have more to do with something Roxie's parents might have been involved with, that she was in the crosshairs because of them, but he couldn't prove it. Not yet.

"Tanya and Monica, you two find anything yet?" Lincoln asked the two PAs he employed, both of whom had left their daughters with Aunt Katie upstairs. As soon as he figured out that Roxie actually had disappeared, he'd had the older woman take Lily out of school and fly up with the two PAs and a security team in tow. The kids were all upstairs, playing dress-up and having a real tea party, thanks to the cook in the house quickly putting together some tea cakes and a pot of weak tea for the children.

"Not yet, Lincoln. I'm doing some research into Matteo's past, not finding much there other than he was married recently. He's stayed pretty much out of the limelight up until now," Monica said and Tanya agreed with a nod.

"I'm not finding anything about Roxie's parents either, Lincoln," Tanya chimed in. "Just the same old thing we always come up with. Marriage certificate, death certificate, a few newspaper pieces on her dad. Nothing else, really." Tanya made a sour face, but Lincoln knew that was because she considered herself a supersleuth when it came to the Internet. If she wasn't finding anything, then it was unlikely anybody else would be able to find much either.

"It's all very strange. In the age when you can pay ten bucks and get anybody's last known address and phone number, all we can find out about any of these individuals is that they were married, went to a few charity events, and that two of them died. There's been some kind of stripping going on here."

Lincoln frowned when Tanya snickered, but she smoothed her face out. She knew what he meant, someone had gone in and stripped out information to protect the privacy of these three individuals. But why? Lincoln could understand Matteo trying to stay lowkey, but why strip out any information about two dead people? It didn't make sense, but that was the truth he was faced with.

"Alright. If we're not going to find any kind of unknown properties, we'll have to stick with the known properties. Have you got team three out at that new address Matteo sent over?" Lincoln's eyes turned to Monica, who nodded pertly.

"Yep, they're going in now, let me just listen in." Monica pointed at the ear bud in her right ear, her eyes going vacant as she listened to the tiny speaker. "Nothing so far. It's another empty building."

"Matteo owns a lot of empty buildings. He should really do something with them," Lincoln mused, but it was just to distract himself while he waited to hear any news that might come in about Roxie. He'd go out himself and look for her, but he was worried he'd be busy storming a building when they found out where she actually was.

For a moment, Lincoln felt a wave of helplessness swamp him. He nearly dropped to his knees as he remembered the last time he'd seen Roxie. Her face was a mask of hurt anger. She'd been…very angry. But he'd seen the hurt beneath that anger. He'd felt it, as if it were his own hurt, and in a way, he had hurt himself when he'd hurt her.

Words, that was all he'd used to hurt her, but they

were hateful words, words meant to sting and dig into her soul. He regretted what he'd done now, he had the moment he'd said them actually. But for now, he needed to focus on getting her back. He could beg her for forgiveness later, when she was safe.

He didn't allow himself to think about the what-ifs, he only thought about the when. When he got Roxie back. When Roxie was safe. When this was all over. Only when all of those whens were reality would he think about anything else. Until then, he'd focus on the things he could do.

Lincoln wasn't surprised when he found himself upstairs, watching his daughter laugh with her friends, through a small opening he'd made when he cracked the door open. Lily had asked him again about her mother when she arrived at the house with Aunt Katie. Her little face had been red from tears and she sniffled as he took her into his arms. He'd told her the only thing he could, that he'd get her mother back to her as soon as he could.

The redness in her cheeks now was from laughter, as Aunt Katie let her and her friends have as many tiny square cakes as they could push into their mouths. They'd all be bouncing off the walls later, but it was a small price to pay to let them all have a moment of laughter. Lincoln pulled the door closed and went back downstairs.

Let her enjoy this moment of innocent fun, he'd deal

with the darker parts of reality for her. Hopefully, he'd have her mother back soon and this would all fade into a strange memory that she couldn't quite remember. He hoped that's how it would turn out anyway.

"Matteo's people found six more properties that should be searched, Lincoln," Monica said as soon as he stepped into the room, and he nodded in understanding.

They were using a study filled with books, tables and chairs for reading, and a large desk as a control center. It hadn't changed since the day Lincoln moved in with his mother all those years ago, instantly gaining a brother. Now he had a half-sister to go with the stepbrother, and both were doing as much as they could.

Liam was helping search the buildings. June was in surgery at the moment, but she'd be back at the house as soon as the patient was settled into a recovery room, helping to trawl through information. Lincoln didn't mind that June was still at work, she was needed there, and her job was important.

He knew both his siblings wanted to help and that was what mattered. Even Dr. Bennet and his soon-to-be new wife were helping by tracking the search teams on a dry-erase board. They were staying in touch with all the teams, marking off properties as they were cleared. They even had Matteo's and Kai's teams up, so there wouldn't be any time wasted with another team searching a building that was cleared already.

It was all very efficient, even if the cops weren't involved. Lincoln had his doubts about the local police and had decided early on that it was pointless to even bring them in when it would only bring questions up. Questions like who Roxie really was, why she was using a fake identity, and what that might mean down the road for her. There were a few mud puddles that would have to be cleared up later, but for now, his focus was on finding Roxie. He had a feeling their sole interest would be in trying to figure out if she'd committed a crime worth pursuing her for before they ever started to look for her.

Nope, best to just leave them out of the loop, right now. And if things went south when they did find Roxie, if someone had to die to get her back, then it was best if the police weren't anywhere around when that happened. Matteo had already assured Lincoln that he and his team would do whatever it took to bring Roxie back safe and sound. Whatever it took, the man had said, with an intensity in his eyes that left little doubt that he meant it.

"Right, what else do we need to do, ladies?" He rubbed his hands together, looking at the dry-erase board on their side of the room.

"I'm sending the new addresses over to Dr. Bennet to coordinate the searches with the teams," Tanya said, typing each address into a message box on the screen of her laptop. "Then I'm going to go through some other files Matteo sent over. There are some properties his uncle owned but the names were never transferred over. He's not sure if he owns them now or if they're in some kind of limbo."

"Those might be exactly what we're looking for." Lincoln moved to stand beside Tanya. "He won't tell me who this person is that he thinks has her, but I have an idea on it. Let's have a look at those addresses. I have a feeling that's where we'll find her."

"Sure, these are the buildings." Tanya frowned as she scrolled through a document file on her screen, and Lincoln leaned to look over her shoulder. "This one is an apartment building. One of my cousins lives near there. I doubt Matteo even knows it exists. My cousin says she won't go near the place because a slumlord owns it. A lot of drugs and prostitution in the vicinity and inside the building."

"Oh?" Lincoln noted the address and typed it into his phone to send to Dr. Bennet as he walked over to the man. "Have we got a team free? I want them to check out this place."

"Hm. An apartment building. We might need to involve the cops with this one. We can't search occupied apartments." Dr. Bennet looked over his black-rimmed glasses to give Lincoln a look that said he didn't like not involving the cops, but he'd do whatever Lincoln asked of him. Because that's what a good dad did. Lincoln sighed heavily, but nodded, the older man would do whatever he asked, but he wouldn't force him to on this one. "No, we don't want to go into validly-occupied apartments. It's the ones that are empty or the ones that are supposed to be empty that we'll search. Without the police, for now."

"As you wish, Lincoln. I know you're suspicious of the local cops but maybe we should contact the police in NYC soon? We're going to run out of legal ways to search if we keep going." Dr. Bennet sighed this time, and Lincoln flattened his lips before he gave another nod.

"I understand, but for now we have Matteo's agreement that we can search the empty buildings and apartments. The man owns a huge chunk of New York City and that's the good news. That means we don't need to involve anybody just yet. Later, if we don't find Roxie, we may need to get the police involved to search a building or two, but for now, we're still within the law. It's fine, really." Lincoln smiled with reassurance, and that seemed to appease the man he respected as the only real father figure he'd ever known.

"That's fine then, son. Let me get a team on this new place." Dr. Bennet turned away to look at the board, picked the one that was closest, and sent the new address to the team leader.

The teams were taking their time, doing a thorough search of each building and the rooms inside. The searches were being done as quickly as possible, though, even if it felt like they were going on forever to Lincoln. The sun had gone down, and his stomach grumbled, but he couldn't think about food right now. Not with Roxie out there somewhere, needing rescue.

He wasn't sure who she needed rescue from or why exactly she'd been taken. Murder was the obvious answer, but he didn't want to think about that. Unfortunately, it was the logical answer he couldn't stomach. Whoever had her wanted her because of the business with Roxie's dad. That was the undeniable link in all of this.

Matteo had tried to call those two men who'd been at Roxie's childhood home that night, but neither had answered the calls. He'd been determined to get them in, to question them and demand answers, but they'd dropped off the face of the Earth. None of Matteo's people knew where the men were either, which meant they'd deliberately dropped out. Not answering the head of the family was a no-no with Matteo's bunch, so it was huge that both men had disappeared.

It meant their allegiance was with someone else and Lincoln suspected they'd pay for abandoning the family long before Matteo could handle that situation. Someone lower down, someone closer to the men, would take care of the betrayal first. If Lincoln didn't get to either one of them before anyone else could. He wanted to break their kneecaps, wanted to crush their spines, and make them pay for what they'd done over the years to Roxie and her family. To his daughter's family.

And if he ever got his hands on any of the people involved, he'd do just that.

11

Roxie

"Please stop," Roxie gasped, her eyes too blurry to see out of, pain a constant piercing ache throughout her body. Blood, sweat, and tears stung at her eyes when she leaned her head to one side or the other, though she wasn't exactly sure which wound the blood was coming from. There were…so many.

In the last couple of hours, the woman had gone silent, but that silence was terrifying. She didn't say a word when she took out what must have been the oldest hair clippers known to man. There wasn't even a cord, so maybe they were meant to be used on animals? Roxie had been terrified when the woman brought the clippers over and held them close to Roxie's lips. The woman had spoken two words then, two words that nearly made Roxie faint.

"Don't move."

She'd then begun to clip away Roxie's hair with the hand-operated clippers, one chunk at a time. Roxie had cried, from fear and from pain. The clippers pulled out more hair than they cut, and the blades had dug into her scalp more than once. There'd been no questions, no demands from the woman, just silent glee that made her appear insane whenever she'd move to look Roxie in the eye.

Roxie had expected some kind of questions, demands for answers, but this was even worse. It was torture for the sake of torture. There were no answers needed, just twisted victory with each clip of those awful metal blades. A thousand possibilities flitted through Roxie's mind, with the main trauma-inducing image being the one where she didn't stop at Roxie's hair. Hair could be regrown, she'd buy a fucking wig if she had to, but what if those blades moved lower?

Roxie wanted to break the cuffs, to find some way out of this, but there was no escape so she tried to stay as still as she could, even when relief flooded through her. That relief didn't last long, though. Major Crazy Bitch just moved on to new and even more delightful torture techniques that did make Roxie pass out once she was done with Roxie's hair.

Roxie didn't move her hands now, not to appease the woman, but because Major Crazy Bitch had pulled all of her fingernails out. Roxie had managed to stay in the real world as the first five were pulled out. It was the other hand that caused her to lose all consciousness. She'd woken up when the woman tried to pull out her toenails, but stopped there for some reason. Roxie tried to breathe through the pain, tried to catch a moment of relief, but the moment didn't last.

She had screamed her throat raw when the first needle was shoved silently under the toenail on her right foot. She wasn't sure, but she thought there were two needles in each of her toes. There'd been no seconds of oblivion with that session, Roxie had endured every moment of it. The woman cackled with joy every time Roxie screamed, as if it were music to her ears. Roxie tried to hold the screams back, wanted to deny the mad woman any kind of pleasure, but she couldn't help it.

Her heart pounded painfully from the pain of the torture, and her pulse raced along in time with her heart. The pounding in her skull was not nearly as painful as the other wounds she now bore, but it didn't help. Roxie writhed from the complete agony she was in, until she accidentally brushed a finger against her head. She went still then, wanting nothing more than a few IVs of morphine and oblivion. She wanted to escape this pain.

But she didn't wish for death. She hadn't wanted to contemplate that being a possibility earlier, but now? Now, she was fairly certain death would be the only out she'd get from this insane woman's torture. Roxie didn't want it to be true, but she had to face facts. This woman was not going to let her go.

It was only when the woman came back into the room that Roxie realized she'd been gone. "I bet all of those little injuries are really starting to throb now, aren't they?"

Roxie didn't respond, she was too afraid to say anything. What if speaking made the woman cut her tongue out? Roxie tried not to roll her eyes in fear, but she allowed the lids to close.

"No, open your eyes, my little beauty. I want you to see what's coming next," the woman said as she grabbed Roxie's chin, making her open her eyes.

Roxie saw a rubber mallet, not a big one, but big enough to cause pain. It seemed the woman's silent period was over as she became a regular chatterbox, spewing a stream of bullshit that Roxie couldn't exactly interpret. "Your father set up Ruby, you know? Yes, the little slut who stole my husband was your dad's cousin and he helped to get her on her feet when she came up here looking to be a star. He introduced her to my husband, MY husband."

The woman struck Roxie with the mallet as she

screamed that last part, hitting her so hard in the hip Roxie was certain the bone had shattered. Roxie jerked on the table, pulling at each of her painful digits, causing pain to explode throughout her body. Roxie screamed again and again, letting the pain wash over her rather than asking the woman to stop again. That had proven pointless anyway.

She'd spent a lot of time in her life treading the line between pleasure and pain, but that had all been voluntary. It had gotten her through the first few nails being pulled out with pliers, but this was prolonged, sustained, unasked for torture. There was no pleasure, there was no satisfaction for her, of any kind. Only the certainty that the woman would not stop until she killed her.

"Now, I could have forgiven your father that part, but he hid her from me after my husband was killed. He took her back down to Louisiana and he hid that swamp trash from me." The woman shrieked every word, and the mallet came down again, aimed right at the lowest part of Roxie's abdomen. It went slightly to the left, almost hitting Roxie's other hip, but it landed all the same.

Roxie began to feel something hot and wet between her legs, but she didn't know if it was blood or urine. It could be either at this point.

"Oh, look. I think you might be losing that monster you're germinating inside of you." The woman dipped her hand between Roxie's legs and pulled her fingers up, covered in blood.

Roxie's blood went cold, but her brain was already taking her away from all of it. She was already a step or two out of the world, barely in it, but unable to let go completely. The pain kept her awake. But her brain was pulling her away.

Don't think about it, Rox. Just focus on breathing, girl. Nothing else, just breathing.

"Oh no, my girl. You aren't going to wander off into some kind of trance on me and escape this little scene. Not going to happen." The woman moved away from the table and came back with a bucket.

"No," but that was all Roxie had time to shout as a bucket of water poured over her head and torso. The woman had left all of Roxie's clothes on, thankfully, but now the clothes held the water against Roxie, freezing her skin in the low temperature.

"Good, I see you're wide awake again. Now, where was I?" The woman picked up the mallet again and looked up at the ceiling. "Oh yes, Ruby and her brat. Because, of course, the stupid slut was pregnant with a baby that should have been mine!"

The woman pouted, her eyes mean and hard, making the pout something nasty.

"I was going to just let it go after that, focus on making a life for myself without my husband. But the woman's brat turned out to be beautiful, and well, I decided I wasn't done with my revenge. You managed to get away from me the night your parents died, and it just seemed like fate wanted me to get rid of that bastard child. So I sent Matteo down there to do the job. He was supposed to destroy the slut and her daughter, but instead, the daughter proved to be just like her mother. I'd raised Matteo from a young boy, you see? He was *my* son. And Ruby's slut of a daughter took him from me. Ruby steals, her daughter steals. Ruby stole my husband, Ruby's daughter stole my boy. I couldn't let that go. But even she keeps escaping me. So I had to focus on you again. And luckily, you made yourself a present to me, didn't you?" The pleased smile was just as blood-chilling as the pout had been, a grimace that Roxie couldn't look away from.

"I have no idea who or what you're talking about," Roxie said when an answer seemed to be needed. "I don't know any of those people."

"No, of course you don't. Your father tried to hide his mother's past. His father made all of his money in oil and left it to him. When my husband was killed your father tried to hide every connection he had to that family, to Ruby, but I knew about them already. Yes, I just tripped right on down memory lane before he managed to erase it all. That's how I found him, found your family. I sent my guys around to teach him some manners when he refused to meet with me, but they botched that, thinking I'd sent them around for money. Then they burned the house down without making sure all of you were in it. So stupid." The woman's words trailed off, but Roxie wasn't really sure any of it made sense anyway.

She sounded crazy, unstable, and obsessed with one too many people. Or happenings. Something. None of it made sense and it was hard to form linear thoughts at the moment, so she stopped trying.

"At least the old slut had the good grace to die," the woman snickered, her eyes shifting from side to side. "Although, I might have helped her along a little. Don't tell anybody that, though. But I guess you won't, will you? If I can't kill my nephew's wife, you'll have to do. Clarence, bring in Charlie, won't you?"

Who the hell was Charlie? Not that Roxie really cared, but if she was about to meet someone else it would have been nice to be prepared. Roxie didn't have to wait long though. As it turned out, Charlie wasn't a who, but a what.

Clarence came in, some kind of contraption in his hands that would surely be ridiculously dangerous in this apartment. Roxie wasn't sure what it was, but it had what looked like a faucet on top and a tank of some kind attached to the bottom of the faucet. There was a vague memory in the back of her mind, a blue flame, but Roxie wasn't sure when the memory was formed or where. It might have even been a movie that she'd seen. Then the woman moved closer and Roxie saw that it was some kind of gas tank that was attached to the brass fitting. Fuck...

"Ah, I see Charlie has your attention. He's my handy-dandy blowtorch. I've only been able to use him a few times since I got him. And he'll take care of any evidence that might be left behind. Have you ever seen a blow-torch in action, my dear? No? Well, you're about to. Clarence, you and Bobby can go. I'll meet you down-stairs in the car." The woman waved the men out of the room and aimed a nozzle at Roxie.

A sound popped in the distance, followed by a dozen or so more.

"What was that?" The woman frowned and went to the door. "Clarence? Bobby? What's going on out there?"

Roxie went still, straining to hear, but no more pops broke the silence. But neither did voices. There was only silence, until a louder pop and a gasp made Roxie turn her head. The woman was on the ground, the blowtorch still clutched in her hand. There was a large hole in the back of her head that Roxie stared at blankly.

I guess that's what happens when a bullet goes through someone's brain then, she thought with detached curiosity.

"Roxie? Are you okay, Roxie?" A voice broke into Roxie's examination of the back of the woman's head, and she smiled when she saw a familiar face in front of her.

"Kai?" Roxie was confused. Why was Kai here?

"It's okay, Roxie, we have you," Kai said with a smile in Roxie's direction. "We need to head straight to the nearest hospital with her."

"We do. Roxie, can you hear me, honey?" The voice she'd longed to hear for hours, days maybe, finally spoke and Roxie turned her head away from Kai.

"Lincoln?" She asked, her eyes narrowing to make sure it was him. She felt the relief of her wrists and ankles being released from the cuffs, but it didn't compare to hearing his voice.

"It's me, baby. We've got you." He threw a blanket over her just before he picked her up. "I'm taking her in my car. Can somebody take care of this mess?"

"I got this, it's the least I can do," a voice that Roxie didn't recognize said, and she looked around to see a handsome man with black hair walking in. He stared down at the woman's body in distaste before he kicked a shoulder. "Yep, that's her. At least this shit is done now."

Roxie's eyes closed but she understood on some level that this must be the boy that the woman was so pissed about. Has she said his name? Roxie didn't know, couldn't stay in the world long enough to remember if she had.

Everything went kind of fuzzy after that.

A few seconds of consciousness told her she was in a car, before she blinked and the world disappeared again. Another moment of awareness and she heard Lincoln's voice explaining he didn't know what had happened, he'd found her like this in a building that was on fire. After that, there were points where she felt pain, a sting here, an ache there, the sensation of more pins in her toes, another needle in her scalp, so many little moments of pain, but then there was oblivion, real oblivion. At least she was still alive. She was fairly certain of that much.

12

Lincoln

"**S**he's what?" Lincoln shouted at his sister, blinking at her with confusion.

"Pregnant. She was going to tell you, but shit kept happening," June said, reverting back to an old habit of swearing when she was uncomfortable.

Lincoln stared at his sister for a long time, not sure how to take this news. "I see."

"You see? You see? Maybe you should tell the fucking doctor, bonehead! If she's bleeding down there, then something is wrong. Tell the damn doctor, Lincoln!" June was all but jumping up and down now, her fury something to witness.

"I will." He put a hand on June's right shoulder. "Don't have a hissy fit. Let me go tell them."

"Finally!" June threw her hands up and went to sit with the rest of the faces in the waiting room, waiting for news about Roxie. June had arrived an hour after he'd brought Roxie into his former step-father's hospital, the only place Lincoln knew he could bring her without too many probing questions.

"Um, excuse me? Nurse? My sister told me Roxie's pregnant," he said when he didn't see the doctor.

"Oh, we know. We do tests on all female patients that need x-rays but aren't conscious. The Ob/Gyn has been in to see her. The baby is fine, there's just some damage to the patient's…" the nurse carried on speaking, but Lincoln didn't hear the rest.

He was too busy looking at Roxie. He didn't know what had happened to her hair but what was left was patchy with a lot of stubble. Her head was covered in cuts, and her face was swollen now. There were bruises underneath both of her eyes, and her bottom and top lip were busted and swollen. Then there was the rest. Her hands and feet were covered in bandages to protect the damaged skin of her nail beds. She'd probably lose all of her toenails, even though the needles beneath them had been removed.

Her right hip was fractured but it was a hairline fracture, nothing the doctor could do there but let it heal. The rest of her was hidden by a white blanket, and Lincoln was almost happy it was there. He hoped the blood had been cleaned away from her. He'd seen it and it had frightened him when they first found her, but the good news was, he was here with her. He could make sure she got the best care available.

There was no doubt the Bennets would ensure that, all three of them. She'd had every exam the hospital could provide, there were three bottles dripping medicine into the IV plugged into her right forearm, and her skin was warm, but not hot. She was as comfortable as she could be.

"I'm here, Roxie," he whispered as he pulled up a chair to sit next to her bed. He took her left hand in his, not wanting to wake her up, but sure that he wanted to touch her. To make sure she was real.

How was he going to explain this to Lily? he wondered. Mommy got a really bad haircut and fell down?

Lincoln frowned, hating any kind of lie, but he'd have to explain something to the girl in a way that wouldn't traumatize her.

And there was another baby on the way?

His heart swelled in his chest, a sensation that took his breath away. Fuck, this was bad. Well, no, it was good, but how was he going to explain this to the guys? He'd sworn he'd never marry or have a girlfriend for so long that even Kai had wondered if he was actually gay a time or two. He'd been adamant about it for so long, but now? He was never going to let her out of his sight again, if he could help it.

If she'd ever forgive him for everything that he'd said the last time they were together. And if she'd forgive what a dick he'd been to her.

"Lincoln? Has she woken up yet?" June's soft voice broke the silence and Lincoln turned his head.

"No, not yet. She needs the rest." Lincoln spoke softly, not wanting to wake Roxie up.

"Okay. Are you hungry?" She waited until he shook his head before she came in and sat down in the chair next to his. "I'll go get you something if you are, you don't have to leave her."

"No, I'm fine. Really. I just want to watch her for a little while." Lincoln's eyes were already on Roxie's bruised and battered face. "If you want to go home, you can. Check on Lily for me. It might be good for her aunt to make an appearance."

"It's still so amazing to me that I'm an aunt." June smiled shyly and looked at Roxie rather than her brother. "She's amazing, you know?"

"Lily or Roxie?" Lincoln asked absently, too busy smoothing out a slight frown that had formed on Roxie's face.

"Both of them." June sighed out the answer, and Lincoln looked back at her. "She's been through so much, but she keeps fighting, doesn't she?"

"She's always been amazing like that," Lincoln answered, thinking about a younger version who went by the name Chloe, who would glare at him angrily and screech at him about how much she hated him. He'd loved her even then, though she hadn't known. He hadn't let himself feel it, not after she ran away, and maybe not when he'd found her again. Oh, his heart had felt what it bloody well wanted to, but he hadn't let himself feel it. He'd tried to fight it. Too bad for him he'd lost that fight.

Or maybe it was the best thing that had ever happened to him. Especially if there was another baby on the way.

"I'll see you at home later. If you come home. I know they're keeping her tonight, so maybe I'll see you in the morning. Try to rest." June put her hand on his head, ran her fingers through his hair for a moment, and blinked away a sudden case of tears. "I love you, big brother. I'm so glad you all found her for us."

"I love you too, little sis. Be careful going home." Lincoln smiled warmly at his sister, one of the few people he could say he loved without feeling like a liar. That circle was expanding now that he'd met Roxie for the second time in his life, he thought, as his sister left. It was a much bigger circle now that included a daughter, a woman as old as his own mother, and a few more.

"June, before you go, can you call her friend Wendy

and tell her what's going on? I'm sure she's worrying. She'll want to know Roxie is okay," Lincoln called out as softly as he could.

"Sure, Lincoln. See you later." June waved as she walked out of the door and left Lincoln alone with the only woman he'd ever loved as a part of himself. "I'm never going to let this happen ever again, Chl…Roxie."

He'd almost called her by her old name. But that wasn't who she was anymore. She was Roxie and always would be, from now on.

She'd earned that name after years of hardship and this shit today. She was like a rock, strong, breakable, but able to make something new out of the pieces that were left. She'd emerge from this as something new, Lincoln knew that, but it would be something that he'd love just as much as he loved her now.

"Lincoln?" Another voice came from the doorway and Lincoln turned to look at the owner.

"Hi, Matteo. How are you?" Lincoln stood up to usher the man out, but Matteo walked in.

"My wife said she'd kill me if I didn't check on her cousin. Marie's stubborn like that, and I believe her when she tells me I'll die." Matteo smiled the smile of men destined to obey their wives on certain whims. "How's Roxie?"

"She's getting there, I guess. The doctor hasn't been in to explain anything yet, and the nurse left soon after I came in. Her vitals look okay, though." Lincoln pointed at the machine and Matteo nodded.

"I won't trouble you too much then. I just wanted you to know we took care of that trouble with my Aunt Celeste. And the two men that worked with her are being handled as we speak," Matteo paused, his face dark and troubled. "I know this doesn't mean much, but she took me from my parents when I was young. Wanted me to take her place when the time came. I knew she was fucked up but had no clue it would get this bad. She's been trying to kill my wife and she went into hiding. I thought she'd run off to Italy and would leave us all alone. If I'd known this would happen, I'd have taken care of her long before today."

"It's not your fault, man. She was unstable, obviously," Lincoln said, still not sure what exactly tied Roxie to Matteo or that woman.

"I suppose you don't know the story. I didn't tell you. It seems my wife's mother was Roxie's aunt. He used to send them money, her father. Marie's mother, Ruth, was my aunt's husband's lover." Matteo looked befuddled for a moment and then nodded. "Yeah, that's right. He wasn't my uncle except by marriage. Anyway, there was bad blood between my aunt and Roxie's family. She wanted me to take over my uncle's family and it made her blow a fuse when I wouldn't end Marie's life. She tried on her own, but, well, we ended up here."

"That sounds like a story you'll need to explain with more detail later, but I know you want to get back to your wife. Thanks for filling me in." Lincoln sat back down in his chair and Matteo took the one beside him, to Lincoln's surprise.

"My, uh, my wife had a question for you, for Roxie when she wakes up." Matteo started but waited for Lincoln to nod before he continued. "She'd like to meet her, meet Roxie that is. They're second cousins, you see? And Marie's family doesn't have a lot to do with her, because of her mother, and she'd like to get to know Roxie."

"I'm sure Roxie will be happy to meet up with any family that she might have, once she's healed up," Lincoln said, not sure that was true, she could be prickly sometimes, but that was a defense mechanism. "I'd like our daughter to have some kind of family too, so we'll arrange something, alright?"

"Yep. That's good. You have my number if you need anything." Matteo stood up with a curt nod of his head. "Take care. I'm sorry we had to meet under these circumstances, but I'm glad it's all over."

"Same here. You go take care of your wife. I'll get in touch soon." Lincoln held his hand out and Matteo shook it with a firm shake before he left.

Well, this day was seriously fucked up, but it was almost over now. And he'd done the one thing he set out to do. He'd brought Roxie home for Lily. And for himself too, he had to admit that, or he'd be a liar. He needed Roxie in his life, needed her like he'd never needed anyone before.

He could admit that now. He'd known it before he thought she was missing but he'd gone about getting her back in his life the wrong way. Maybe saving her from a torturous early death wasn't the best way either, but he hoped she'd listen to him, once she woke up and had time to recover.

"What's going on?" Her sleepy voice had him looking up instantly. He hadn't realized his head had fallen, her hand once again in his.

"You're in the Bennet's hospital, Roxie. Everything is okay." He spoke with calm, hoping to relay the best information first.

"Everything?" She asked, pulling her hand away from his to look at the bandages. "How can they still fucking hurt so much?"

"Shit, sorry. I didn't even think about your nail beds." He felt his cheeks flush and guilt gnawed at him.

"No, I think it's the bandages. They feel like they're throbbing." Her voice grew faint, and her eyes closed again. "And that woman?"

He'd thought she was falling back asleep, but her question disproved that. "That woman is dead, honey."

"Good." She gave a short nod before her eyes opened

again, slightly out of focus but present. "I'm glad that's over with then. Will I have to answer a bunch of questions?"

"No, we're in the Bennet's hospital. There aren't any police involved." Lincoln looked around but couldn't see anyone. It might be his family's hospital, but that didn't mean they could speak freely forever. "We still need to keep some of this stuff to ourselves until you're out of here, honey."

"That's fine with me. If I don't ever have to think about any of it again, that'll be just fine." Her eyes closed again, and she took a deep breath. "And has the doctor told you anything, Lincoln?"

"About the baby you mean?" He asked tentatively, worried she'd be upset that he knew. He knew she was when she made a sour face at his question. "He didn't, June did before the doctor could."

"For fuck's sake. Yes. I wanted to tell you. I wanted to be the one who told you this time." She paused, tears filling her eyes. "Shit happened."

"Yes, that's exactly what June said. You mean I happened. I'm sorry about all of that, by the way. I won't be ripping your daughter away from you. I shouldn't have been such a dick to you, even if I was pissed. This is probably something I should save for later, but I promised myself I'd apologize to you as soon as I could. And I mean it, Rox. I'm really sorry about everything."

"We can talk about it all later, Lincoln. I just want to close my eyes for now, okay? I don't hate you, I'm just so tired." She looked incredibly sad, and he had to wonder if she was saying more than she wanted to right now.

"Sure, yeah. Later's good." He nodded like an idiot, completely terrified now that later would bring a heartache unlike anything he'd ever felt before.

"Thanks, Lincoln. For saving me, for understanding. For everything." Her eyes closed then and he wanted to beg her to stay awake but that would just be selfish. She needed to rest. Later she could break his heart, if that's the choice she'd made after all of this. And who could blame her if she had? He deserved it, really.

13

Roxie

The pain had receded, but the memories of that night were still too fresh. It had completely shaken Roxie that she'd set a trap for herself like that. That crazy bitch hadn't had to do anything. Roxie, certain in her fierce independence and capabilities, had made herself a prize that could not be resisted, and that had shaken her belief in everything she thought she knew about herself.

They were all still in the Bennet children's mansion, but Roxie was in her own room this time. She shared that room with Lily most nights, unwilling to let the child sleep in her own room. It wasn't fair to Lily since Roxie often woke up from nightmares, but she did all she could to keep from waking her daughter. Lily didn't know exactly what had happened, none of them had been quite willing to explain it in detail to the little girl, but she knew her mother had been in an accident and was recovering.

Roxie didn't keep Lily in her room at night for moral support though, she kept her there to make sure she was safe. That crazy bitch, Celeste, Roxie now knew her name was, had threatened Lily next. And even though she'd seen the hole in the back of the woman's head, even though Lincoln reassured her every day that the woman was nothing but ashes now, Roxie woke up every night reaching for Lily.

It was another morning in New York. Later in the day, Lincoln was taking Lily, Aunt Katie, and Roxie back to Myrtle Beach, but for now, Roxie had a meeting to get through. She looked at the faded bruises beneath her eye, the faint line of one of the splits in her lip, and decided makeup wasn't worth bothering with.

She was about to meet a stranger. A distant cousin, but still a stranger. And apparently one of the reasons Celeste was so damned crazy. The child of Celeste's dead husband and the woman who'd turned his head was on the way to visit her. They had more in common than that since Celeste had admitted to trying to kill Marie too.

Roxie had spoken with her on the phone but hadn't met her yet.

"I think this is the one you wanted." June came into Roxie's room without a knock, the formality unnecessary between the two friends, especially when the door was already open. In her hands, June carried a box without a name, just a symbol.

The symbol didn't matter. What was inside did. "Let me see?"

Roxie smiled at her friend and took the box once June had removed the gold lid. Inside was a wig, a blonde wig, a chin-length bob that was out of character for Roxie. It was girlish though, and fun. Something that Roxie needed more of, especially while her hair grew back, and her scalp recovered. It would be a long time before she could do anything but let her hair grow, and what had already started to creep out of her skull was blonde, so Roxie decided to keep up the trend with a blonde wig that June had gone out to the boutique to buy for her.

"Can you put it on?" June asked as Roxie lifted the wig out and started to lift it.

"I think so, I just have to watch these stitches. They're coming out later, thank goodness." Roxie grimaced a little as the wig touched a particularly sensitive stitch, but she clipped the hooks at the back without removing the wig.

"Let me see, I've watched some videos about these. And the owner of the boutique did some work on it to make it look realistic. We have to cut this netting here, and you can use glue to make sure it doesn't move once the stitches are out and everything's healed." June twitched at the wig until it looked right to her, then picked up some nail scissors from the table. "Want me to do the cutting?"

"Please." Roxie smiled up at her friend, glad to have one so eager to help her out in a matter so personal.

Hair was just hair, and that's what she'd told herself as Celeste massacred her head, but now? Hair was a huge part of her identity and it stung that all that remained under the wig was stubble and scars. She couldn't even look pretty now that her face had healed, not without the wig.

"There, what do you think about that? I added some baby hairs around your forehead, just to make it look more real." June stepped back and Roxie looked in the mirror.

The hair was human hair, so it didn't have the fake sheen of cheaper synthetic wigs, and it was styled perfectly. It was kind of hot on her head, but she'd have to get used to that. Maybe when more of her own hair grew out she'd be brave enough to walk outside without a wig on, but for now, she needed something to hide behind. Even if the wig was a short bob style. "It looks amazing. Thank you."

"Anything for you, you know that." June looked

down at Roxie, her eyes noting what had healed, but she didn't comment on anything. "When's Marie coming?"

"She'll be here in twenty minutes or so. Do you want to meet her?" Roxie didn't mind if June did want to meet her newly-found cousin, she'd just like a private chat first.

"Sure, after you two talk, of course. I know there's stuff you need to talk about." June looked down at her pale hands, but then looked back up, as if forcing herself to let go of her girlish shyness. "I'd love to meet her, actually."

"Cool. Then you shall, my friend. How's Lily?" Roxie stood up and moved to put on the dress draped on the back of the chair she'd been sitting in. Up until now, she'd been wearing matching underwear and a silk robe. She slipped the robe off and pulled the black sweater dress on over her head. Her nail beds had healed enough that they didn't hurt, but there were still no nails on her fingers.

Her toes were problematic because the nerves beneath the nails had been abused. Several nails had already fallen off so wearing socks or hose was next to impossible. Add in the vague pain that came with shoes and Roxie was limited in what she could put on her feet. Lincoln had bought her a pair of Uggs with a lot of width at the toes and that was about all she could wear at the moment. She'd always hated wearing socks, but this was actual pain that made even the thought of sliding them over her toes cringe-inducing. She slid on the black leather boots very carefully and turned to look in the mirror. June and the woman at the boutique had done such a fine job, even Roxie had a hard time telling the hair on her head was a wig. She twisted and turned her head, but the wig stayed in place, even when she shook her head vigorously.

"Lily's fine, excited to go on a plane again," June said once Roxie was changed and in her boots. "She's also excited since I kind of promised I'd take her to Disneyland next summer."

"You didn't!? Roxie turned with a laugh, mock-glaring at Lily's favorite, if only, aunt. "You're all going to spoil her beyond belief."

"That's what we're for, my love," June said, looking down her nose with a grin. "We're here to spoil her so she'll know just how much we love her."

"Love isn't a present," Roxie said, only half-kidding. She was glad Lily's family wanted to spoil her, but she didn't want the girl to think objects equaled love at all. "It's wanting to give a present, it's wanting to make someone's wishes come true. That's the part that's real love, June."

"I know, I'm sorry." June's cheeks turned red, and Roxie felt bad instantly.

"No, you're right. Every now and then Lily should

have something nice. I just don't want her to come to expect it. I won't raise a spoiled brat," Roxie said, her hand going to her stomach. The baby was still there, safe and sound, despite the abuse Celeste had doled out to her. "Or two, as it so happens."

"Everything okay, there?" June glanced at Roxie's stomach but quickly looked away. "Any more bleeding?"

"No, everything's fine, really." Roxie looked away, tucking a lock of the wig behind her ear as a way to distract them both. "How's that?"

"Can't tell a thing, honey," June reassured her, before she got up off of Roxie's bed and went to the door. "I'll see you downstairs when you're ready for me to meet your cousin. I'll keep Lily busy with the new puzzle I got her."

"Another gift?" Roxie blew air at the top of her head and rolled her eyes.

"Yes, but I still love you, bestie," June called out, doing a prancing dance out of the doorway.

"And I still love you too, bestie," Roxie called back with a smile.

This meeting might be making her tense, but June was doing her best to make her smile and relax. Lincoln was out taking care of some last-minute things before they all left later. She hadn't spoken much with him since that night, she didn't know what to say. There was a lot for her to deal with at the moment, and he was a complicated situation. Very complicated now that he knew about the new baby on the way.

He hadn't pushed, he'd been as patient as a saint, but there were questions in his eyes. Questions she didn't know the answers to because she'd had to question everything she believed about herself. There was a doubt in her ability to make decisions, to keep her and her daughter safe, that had really rattled her.

And on top of that, she could reclaim her old identity, at last. But did she really want to be the person she used to be? Did she want to be Chloe Abshire again when Roxie Sinclair was...well, before Celeste, she'd have said she was a badass, capable of taking care of herself. Now?

Not so much.

Chloe certainly wouldn't have been able to handle being tortured like that. But, wasn't she Chloe, deep down inside? As she walked down the stairs to wait in the living room for her guest, Roxie wondered if she was doing herself a disservice. She tended to think of herself before the night of the fire as weak, spoiled, and incredibly naïve. The woman she'd become, the persona of Roxie that she'd created, had been borne from her struggles to make ends meet after giving birth to a child she had no idea how to take care of as Chloe.

Roxie frowned deeper, wondering if she was the crazy one here. You can't be two people, even if you changed your name. She was the girl who used to think she was in love with Liam. She was also the woman who knew she loved Lincoln.

That didn't mean she was good enough for Lincoln though. What if she got another stupid idea in her head and put herself in danger again? Or worse, one of the children, once this baby was born? She couldn't be trusted to make decisions beyond which wig to buy, she knew that much.

"Miss Roxie, your guest has arrived," one of the staff said as she escorted a pretty, black-haired woman into the living room.

"Hi, I'm Marie," the woman said with an accent that Roxie couldn't quite define. She knew it must be the Cajun accent Marie grew up with, but it was unlike anything Roxie had ever heard. It wasn't a northern accent, but it wasn't quite southern either. What it was, Roxie decided, was charming, much like the young woman that came with the accent.

"Hi, I'm Roxie. Chloe." Roxie waved her hands with a roll of her eyes.

"Which do you prefer?" The woman with dark brown eyes and clear skin asked. She was very pretty, Roxie noted, admiring her cousin's dark good looks. And she was considerate too, how wonderful.

"I prefer Roxie, thanks. Would you like a drink?"

Roxie asked and made a motion to a tray on the coffee table.

"Just water, please." Marie came to sit beside Roxie on the white couch. Roxie knew the woman was nervous from the way she sat on the edge of the couch, despite the fact that she'd used a cane to walk in.

Roxie hadn't noticed it at first, the white cane blended in with the woman's white pants and white sweater perfectly. But now that the woman was seated the cane was hard to miss.

Roxie filled a glass with water and handed it to her new cousin. "This is a strange way to find out about each other, isn't it?"

"Yes, it is. I mean, I knew there was someone who helped my mother pay the bills for a while, but then it stopped, and things got, well, kind of bad." Marie's eyes moved everywhere but to meet Roxie's. "My mother was really good at pushing people away. She'd had a taste of fame and the good life, and she wasn't a very pleasant woman, to put it nicely."

"I'm sorry, but I do wish I'd known about you. I grew up thinking I had no family at all. Well, there's some kind of aunt in Paris, but I've never met her either." Roxie's words trailed off. This was awkward, but she was determined to get her and the other woman through it with ease if she could. "You, um, your mother is dead now, right?"

"She is. She had Parkinson's. I have it too, but I'm taking a new medicine. It's working to keep me going, so far." Marie smiled an easy smile. "Knowing I won't be a target for assassination has helped too."

"Yes, I suppose it would." Roxie's eyes went wide, but then she looked away. "That awful woman damaged so many lives."

"She did. My poor Matteo, he grew up with a vicious cow as a mother figure. He still can't say if he ever loved her. She was all he had though. She raised him to take over the family business."

"He's part of the, um, Mafia, isn't he?" Roxie felt like that might be a stupid question, but she was curious.

"Yeah, technically, he's not a part of the Alfonsi family, but they all accept him as the head of the family. They all love him and I guess it's okay. Especially now that she's gone." Marie didn't have to mention which woman she meant, Roxie knew. "But that also means that you're free to live your life now, too."

"It does, yeah," Roxie agreed with a polite smile, not sure how much to ask or share with this woman. She seemed sweet, nice, too innocent to be in with the Mafia, but she'd just admitted it. "Wow, that must be totally different from your old life."

"Not really. There's still the family squabbles, family politics, all of that to deal with. Before my mother ran everyone off, we had a big family. It's no different to navigating all of those minefields really," Marie said, then sighed. "I'm sorry this is so awkward for us both."

"No, we can blame our families for that. But I'm glad you wanted to meet me. That's a good start." Roxie tried to alleviate some of the worry on Marie's face. The woman was obviously a worrier and Roxie wanted to ease that. Especially if she was ill. "Would you like to meet my daughter and her aunt?"

"I'd love to," Marie said with relief. The private conversation hadn't lasted long, but it was long enough for both women to know that they wanted to meet up again. "It's nice to know I have some family of my own left. Matteo's family is large, and I love most of them dearly, but…they aren't *my* family."

"I know what you mean. I've been on my own for over ten years now. It's nice to know I'm not alone anymore. Maybe you and your husband can come down to visit us in Myrtle Beach later this year." Roxie stood up, paused, and then spoke again. "Or we can come to you."

"Maybe both? That would be nice." Marie smiled happily and Roxie went to get her daughter and June. When she came back into the room, Marie was still on the couch, looking relaxed and happy.

"Marie, this is my daughter, Lily, and her aunt, June. Say hello, Lily." Roxie held Lily, suddenly shy, by the shoulders, but her hands moved up to trace down her daughter's hair. Lily looked up at her mother before she turned back to look at Marie.

"Hello. I'm Lily. It's nice to meet you," Roxie heard Lily say, her voice soft and gentle.

"Hi, Lily. I'm Marie. I'm your third cousin." Marie smiled at the girl, her eyes steady and calm. This seemed to reassure Lily and Roxie felt her daughter move. Lily pulled away to walk up to Marie, her eyes curious, her head tilted to the side.

"What's a third cousin? Who are my other two?" Lily asked and Roxie had to stifle a laugh. She didn't want to embarrass the girl, so she just smiled and went to sit in a chair to the side of the couch.

"No, honey, that's not what it means," Marie said with patience and kindness. Roxie appreciated the way Marie spoke to her daughter. "It means that your mom and I are second cousins. Let me explain it like this, June is your aunt, right?"

Roxie watched as Lily nodded, wondering if the child would understand the simple, yet overly complex way of noting relations.

"Well, if your aunt had a baby, that baby would be your cousin. And when you grow up, if you and your cousin have children then those children would be second cousins. That's what your mom and I are. So, you and I are third cousins." Marie looked uncertain, thought about it for a moment, and seemed to decide that was right.

"I think that's right, Marie. It should be simple, but it's kind of complicated without a pen and a piece of paper." Roxie laughed gently and looked over at June. "Can you add anything to that?"

"No, believe me. I get confused with it all, still, and it's been explained to me dozens of times. Especially when you add in that 'once removed' and 'twice removed' nonsense." June rolled dark brown eyes and looked at Marie. "It's nice to meet you, by the way."

"And you." Marie blushed and looked down at her lap, clearly a shy woman who was trying her best to not embarrass herself.

"I'm still not sure what all of that means, but I guess it means we're related, right?" Lily asked, and Roxie could see she wanted to be friends with the woman. That was good. "Like my dad's mom is Aunt June's mom, but she isn't my Uncle Liam's mom. And Papa George isn't my real grandfather, but he'd be Aunt June and Uncle Liam's babies' grandfather?"

"A bit like that, honey," Roxie said, smiling a wobbly smile as she thought about the complications that came with broken relationships. Lily would get used to the confusion and come to accept her family as it was. Roxie knew that, but still, she knew if her relationship didn't work out with Lincoln, the map of Lily's relations could become even more complicated. A new baby would complicate all of that more, but there was nothing Roxie could do about that. She wanted this baby as much as she'd wanted Lily.

"I'll figure it all," Lily said with a laugh and reached out to touch Marie's long black hair. "I love how shiny your hair is. It looks so soft."

And just like that, all of the women in the room finally relaxed, even if Roxie felt a twinge of regret that her own hair had been shorn with such brutal force. Hair would regrow and hopefully, as her hair grew, so would her relationship with this new cousin.

14

Lincoln

$\mathcal{H}$e watched his daughter and her mother sleep, nestled together on a couch in the private plane Kai insisted he use to take his small family back to South Carolina. Lily was fine, healthy, and full of life, but Roxie was pale and seemed to be...slightly broken.

Hardly a surprise, considering what she'd been through. The most obvious signs on her face had started to heal, but she'd covered her head with a wig, hiding the torture she'd been put through. The short blonde hair suited her, but it still made his heart ache. He knew it was a wig, knew what was under it, and it reminded him of how he'd failed her.

Yes, he and Kai, along with everyone else, had

finally figured out where she was, had taken the steps necessary to save her, but she'd been through hell before they arrived. She still hadn't spoken about the woman or what had happened with her. If June was being honest, Roxie hadn't spoken with her about it either.

Lincoln had considered enlisting the help of a professional, but he'd put it off. Roxie needed time to heal, physically, mentally, and emotionally. She'd ask for help if she needed it. He knew that much about her. But what if that experience had changed her, had made it impossible for her to ask for help?

He'd contact someone down there at the beach. That was where she lived, it was the place she considered home. He'd give her a few days to settle back into life, to heal a little bit more, then he'd insist she speak with some kind of therapist. She'd been tortured, after all. Kidnapped and tortured.

It still made him want to go back in time and kill that woman slowly and painfully, but he couldn't do that. He had managed to get a little vial from Matteo, filled with the woman's ashes. It was a macabre token, but he wanted to keep part of her with him, to prove that she was gone, to show her that all of her efforts were for nothing, if any part of her still existed in the world. Lincoln wasn't the kind of man that believed in ghosts, but he almost hoped that Celeste was a ghost now, attached to that vial, and helpless to stop the life that went on without her.

Lily moved on the couch, gently pulled away from her mother, and came to sit on Lincoln's lap where she wrapped her arms around his neck. She was squishy and warm, all things cuddly and childlike, he thought, as he wrapped his arms around the little girl. "Are you alright, honey? We'll be landing soon."

"I'm okay, Daddy. I'm just worried about Mommy. She's so pale now and she's always so sad. Even when she smiles, she still looks sad. Did I do something to make her sad?" Lily's face was pressed into Lincoln's neck so he pulled her away so he could look at her.

"No, honey, you didn't do anything wrong at all. Somebody, well, somebody hurt Mommy, but it wasn't you. And that person can never hurt anyone again." Lincoln wondered if he'd revealed too much there, but when he saw the look on Lily's face, he decided he hadn't been wrong. That fierce look of satisfaction didn't belong on a child's face, but it was a look Lincoln was familiar with. He'd often had it on his own face over the years. Yep, this was his baby girl.

"I'm glad they can't hurt anyone anymore. Will Mommy stop being sad soon?" Lily settled down in his lap and leaned against his chest, relaxed with her father. That touched him deep in his heart and he put his hand out to cup her face.

"She will, honey. I hope so, anyway. I don't like seeing Mommy sad either." Lincoln sighed and sat back in the chair with Lily. "We'll get some help for Mommy if we need to, but right now, she just needs to rest."

His eyes were on Roxie, still asleep with a blanket over her torso. She still could barely stand to have anything on her toes, even socks. She had on a pair of men's socks that were much too large, just to keep her feet warm, but they didn't touch her toes with any kind of pressure. He wondered how long it would take before she could stand anything on her toes. The doctor had said a couple of weeks, perhaps, but Lincoln had a feeling it might be longer. He wondered if some of the pain Roxie felt was mental, but he didn't want to suggest it. She might take it as him diminishing her pain or insulting her, and he wasn't trying to do that at all. He just wanted to…protect her. Even if it was already too late to protect her from the worst that had happened to her.

"Aunt June is going to take me to Disneyland next summer," Lily said after a few minutes of silence.

"I've heard. Are you sure you want to go that far without your mom?" Lincoln asked, wondering if she'd still want to go if Roxie didn't go. He still had no idea how far along Roxie was in her pregnancy, but the summer months would surely find her giving birth and with a newborn. Roxie may not want to travel if she had a baby to take care of.

"Would you stay with Mommy?" Lily asked, deep concern pulling her eyebrows together.

"If she wanted me to, yes, honey. I'll always take care of your mom, if she'll let me," he answered honestly, while also letting Lily know it was her mother's decision to make. It was important that she understand a man should take a woman's wishes into consideration.

"Good. Mommy needs you to take care of her," Lily said, and Lincoln could only hug her tight for a second before he let her go.

"Come on, get in your seat. We'll be landing soon." Lincoln pushed her gently towards her seat and buckled his own seatbelt.

Roxie sat up and got in her own seat, making Lincoln wonder if she'd heard his discussion with Lily. She didn't act like she'd heard anything, instead, she smiled at him, touched her wig to make sure it was still in place, and then made sure Lily was comfortable.

Lincoln watched her, feeling a distance there that he couldn't close. She'd kept him at arm's length since she got out of the hospital. She'd speak to him, discuss Lily with him, but she balked at conversations about their relationship or about the baby on the way. He hadn't tried to push her on the subject, not yet, but soon she'd have to say something, one way or another.

Either their relationship was done and he needed to move on, or she needed to let him back into her life. He wasn't concerned about sex, or the lack of it, he wasn't even sure if there was ever going to be sex between them again, but he did want to know if he could love her or not. There was always loving her from afar, he thought, with a silent roll of his eyes, but if they were done he wanted to know. That was all.

And maybe being his again would help to heal her. Wasn't love supposed to help heal deep invisible wounds like hers? There was the new baby and Lily, who could probably heal all of her wounds, but he'd like to be a part of that healing. If she wanted him to be.

The plane landed and Lincoln drove them all back to his house, with a stop to pick up Chinese food for dinner. Aunt Katie had some business to take care of and would be flying back down to Myrtle Beach in a couple of days. For now, it was just the family that Lincoln hadn't known he wanted more than anything he'd ever wanted before. Not until he'd almost lost one of the most important members of that family.

"Who wants an egg roll?" Lincoln asked as he dug out bags of egg rolls, crab Rangoon, and boxes filled with the dishes they'd ordered. Roxie remained silent but Lily jumped up and down with excitement.

"I want an egg roll and crab ragoo," Lily said, unable

to pronounce the Rangoon part in such a sweet way it made Lincoln laugh.

"You can have both, honey. Hand me your plate." Lincoln doled out food to them all, watching Roxie, who'd barely said a word since she got on the plane earlier. "Roxie? You hungry or do you want to wait?"

"I'll just have my sesame chicken, please." She looked up at him for a second, then looked back at her plate. Her eyes were haunted, and he knew she'd been back in that dark place for a second. A second that probably felt like an eternity to her.

"I think you should have some crab ragoo, as Lily calls it. I know it's one of your favorite things." He'd ordered extra, just because of that.

"Oh, sure. Yeah." She blinked and nodded in agreement, as if suddenly coming back to life. "Lily, don't eat too much, baby. You'll be sick if you eat all of that fried rice."

Lincoln looked over to see Lily had scooped out a huge pile of rice onto her plate. It was far more than she could eat, but he'd let her try, if she wanted to. "It's okay, Roxie. Let her have a try."

"Oh. Okay." Roxie looked down at her plate, and he knew he'd done something wrong, but he didn't know what. If only he knew how to make this all better for her, he would. But he couldn't, and that killed him a little bit every day.

15

Roxie

It wasn't that they were back in Lincoln's house that had Roxie inwardly panicking. It was that room upstairs. A room where she'd been given, and had given pleasure, that made her want to grab her bags and her daughter and run away.

It was illogical and she knew it, but just knowing that room was there, knowing that there was a massage table, handcuffs, all kinds of ties and binds, made her skin crawl. She knew it was her own issue, that Lincoln would not mention that room, or anything else that might upset her. Just as she knew he wouldn't take her anywhere near that room. What had happened in that room was nothing like what had happened to her in New York, but it was still too much of a reminder.

She just couldn't say that to him. There was no way to explain it to him, how she felt being so close to that room. He'd said to her, before she left his house that day, that he was taking over custody of Lily, so if she wanted to be near her daughter now, and she very much wanted to be as close to Lily as she could be, then she'd have to stay with Lincoln. Despite that room. Despite the fear that tried to claw its way up her throat the minute she walked in the door and remembered that room upstairs.

On some level, Roxie knew this was trauma, knew it was desecrating the memory of the things they'd shared in that room. There wasn't anything she could do about it, though. Saying anything to him might cause an argument, might end with him telling her to go back to her own apartment, but she'd have to go without Lily.

In the end, she'd decided to keep her trap shut and not say anything. This was her issue. She'd have to deal with it on her own. "I'm going to lie down for a little while."

"Sure. I'll stay down here with Lily. You rest, Rox." Lincoln nodded but she caught the look of disappointment on his face and the way he frowned at her full plate. She'd only eaten a little of her food, but her stomach was twisted up and she couldn't force even some of her favorite foods down her throat. She'd heat it up later if she got hungry.

Roxie walked up to the room that was hers and

turned the TV on, just to have some noise in the room. She undressed, avoiding her still-tender toes as much as she could. Her fingertips were still a little tender, but not as much as her toes were. Part of her was afraid the pain would never go away, that there'd be a constant reminder of her time spent with that awful woman, but she habitually crushed that part of her thinking.

She picked a movie that seemed light, funny even, put on a baby pink nightgown, and got under the covers. She closed her eyes as the duvet settled over her, feeling almost at home for a peaceful second. This was what she'd needed, a quiet place with few people in it. Even if that room was down the hall, locked to everyone but Lincoln.

The opening credits of the movie ended, and Roxie turned to watch it. The movie played on, absorbing all of Roxie's attention until someone knocked at the door. Her body stiffened, but she didn't move. It could only be Lincoln or Lily, but fear still traced through her veins, polluting the peaceful shield she'd built around herself.

"Hey, it's Lincoln. Your phone started buzzing, do you want it with you?" He asked through the door.

Roxie stayed silent, hoping he'd assume she was asleep. She waited, breath held, but he moved away from the door. Her eyes moved back to the television, letting her brain become absorbed in the movie again.

It wasn't fair to him, this wall she'd put between him.

It wasn't the things he'd said to her before she'd left for New York that had erected that wall. It was her experience with Celeste, and her own doubt in herself. He didn't need someone as broken as her in his life, not as a romantic partner, anyway. And she couldn't let herself… she wasn't sure what the word was.

She loved him already, that wouldn't change. She trusted him. Knew he'd done everything he could to find her, to save her. June had told her everything that had happened. And it wasn't that she was afraid to be happy, either. She just couldn't take the thought of intimacy, not when it meant giving up control of herself.

Understanding blossomed in her mind at last, and the movie faded away.

Celeste had taken every bit of her autonomy, her self-control. The woman had shown her that everything she thought was true wasn't. Civility was an illusion that could be shattered with a pair of clippers, or a pair of pliers. The idea that you could determine what happened to you, with you, had disappeared when that woman violated Roxie's body with needles that she pushed into Roxie's toes.

Thank fuck they'd found her before she could go to work with that blow torch, but even knowing that she'd been saved hadn't stopped the nightmares. Nightmares that brought to life what would have happened if Kai and Lincoln hadn't found her, hadn't saved her.

Her own brain was causing her more trauma after the fact.

Roxie felt something wet on her face and realized she was crying. She hadn't really cried before, a few tears here and there, but now that she was alone, really alone, she couldn't stop the tears. And when she started to sob out huge gasping sobs into the pillow, she couldn't stop those either.

A snick at the door wasn't enough to stop the tears or the sobs, not until a tiny pair of arms went around her waist and a much larger hand cupped her cheek.

"Please don't cry, Mommy," Lily said against the back of her head.

"Cry it out if you have to, Rox," Lincoln said from across the bed, his feet still on the floor. Only Lily had crawled into the bed with her. Lincoln had respected her enough to not get on the bed with her. Still, he wanted to comfort her, wanted to let her do what she needed to and that mattered.

She opened her eyes to look at him. She saw how concerned he was, how he wanted to do more but wouldn't, not unless she wanted him to. All she could muster was a watery smile, but that soon turned stronger. "It's okay, I'm better now."

"Are you sure?" He asked, kneeling down on that side of the bed, but still not in it.

"Yeah." She nodded, putting a hand over Lily's much

smaller one as he pulled his hand back from her face. "I just had a moment, that's all."

"Want to talk about it?" He asked, but she shook her head.

"No, not right now. Maybe later." She indicated Lily with a slight nod of her head.

Lincoln didn't look overly pleased with that, but even if she did actually talk to him about all of this, it wouldn't happen with Lily in the room. Maybe not in this house, with that room in it.

"Want me to sleep with you tonight, Mommy?" Lily asked, crawling over Roxie's body to look her mother in the face.

"If you want to, baby." Roxie smiled at Lily, brushing her hair behind her ear. "If you want to sleep in your room, though, you can."

"I don't mind staying in here with you, Mommy. I know you have the bad dreams, and I don't want you to wake up alone," Lily said, wisdom beyond her years coming out in a way that surprised Roxie.

"Thank you, honey, but I'll be okay. I will, I promise." Roxie knew she'd interrupted Lily's new routine enough. It was time her daughter had some kind of normalcy back. There was a security team outside, even if all the threats against Roxie had been neutralized. Lincoln would never allow another night to go by without actual people watching out for them all. Lily would be safe in her room.

"If you're sure, Mommy. Can I watch Stephanie until I fall asleep?" Lily asked, and Roxie agreed. Stephanie was a science cartoon character for young girls, a cartoon that Roxie could definitely appreciate.

"Thanks, Mommy." Lily kissed her mom and jumped off the bed. No doubt to run to her room and turn the TV on.

"Are you sure you'll be okay, Rox?" Lincoln prodded, making Roxie turn her eyes to him.

"I'm having a rough time right now. I'll be alright soon. I promise." Her smile was a little too flat, but it was all she could muster at that moment.

"Do you want to talk to a professional?" Lincoln asked, his eyes on his hands, not her. He didn't want her to feel shame about any of it, she could sense that.

"Maybe, yes. It might be best." She had to acknowledge it at some point. She'd been through hell and might need some help dealing with that. It was one thing talking to your lover or best friend, but a professional could help in ways that the others couldn't. A therapist had the tools and skills to help her through this.

"I'll find one for you tomorrow then. I'll get the best I can find." He stood back up, but stepped away from the bed. He was being extra careful to not make her feel threatened, which she appreciated, even if she couldn't say it out loud.

"Thank you, Lincoln." The words came out woodenly, but that couldn't be helped either. She was on the verge of bursting out in tears again, and she simply didn't want to. Not because he was there but because she hated how weak she felt when she cried.

"I'll leave you, then. If you need me, you know where I am." He stepped away, but paused at the door. "Even if I'm asleep, Rox, please wake me up if you want me. I know things are weird between us right now, but I will always be here for you, however you need me."

"Thanks. That means a lot to me." She couldn't look him in the eye though, mainly because she couldn't say the same back. She wasn't sure she could say that to anyone but her daughter and unborn baby right now.

"Good night," he said and closed the door on his way out.

Roxie stared at the door for a long time, but she didn't get up. Instead, she put another movie on, an old one about a hospital with a lot of coma patients, and fell asleep. For the first time since she'd woken up in the hospital, she slept peacefully and without nightmares.

When she woke up the next morning, Lincoln was making breakfast for Lily and getting her ready for school.

"Hi, Roxie. Listen, you have two doctor appointments today," he said, sliding a paper with names, times, and addresses on them. "I have to work, but if you want me to go with you to either, I will."

"Okay, what's the first one?" She asked, noting the name but not seeing what each doctor was for.

"B-A-B-Y doctor," Lincoln spelled the word out, making Lily roll her eyes.

"I can spell, Daddy. Mommy's not a baby, why does she need a baby doctor?" Lily asked, frowning.

"Because sometimes mommies need to see them," Lincoln said, which wasn't really an answer, but Lily accepted it.

"Okay. Do you want to go to that one?" Roxie waited for him to answer. He nodded, shooting her a glance that said he really wanted to go. "Alright, you can come. The second one?"

He looked at her steadily for a few seconds. "I'll take you if you need the moral support. I think you'll want to do that one alone, don't you?"

That was the therapist then. "If you want to come to the first appointment, that's fine. And you can drive me to the second one."

"That's fine," he answered her with a slight smile.

It was a step, a small one, but still a step.

At least he had the sense to know she needed help with all of this. He hadn't made her feel bad, or like she was crazy, he'd just accepted that all of this was bigger than either of them and he'd done what needed to be done. He was still taking charge, but at least it was in a proper direction.

And he'd also had his own experience with kidnapping, Roxie thought, as he bundled Lily up with her schoolbag and took her off to school. Nathan had kept him locked in a storage unit for days, and he'd managed to shake it all off. Or it seemed he had, anyway.

Perhaps that was why he'd demanded total custody of Lily, it was his way of taking back his control. And perhaps that's why he'd acted like such a dick to Roxie when he found out about Lily, something else that had been decided without his consent. Roxie had kept Lily a secret from him, taking away more of his control. Which was no excuse to be a dick to her, seeing as how she'd only done that to protect him, but she hadn't quite explained that well, if she remembered it all correctly.

The last few weeks before her trip to New York were kind of a blur. She looked at the first name on the paper and wondered what the doctor would say. When she was in the hospital in New York, an ultrasound hadn't been able to determine exactly how far along she was, other than maybe three months, maybe four. June hadn't been certain, though she'd tried her best.

When Roxie sat down to try to think of exactly when she might have gotten pregnant, all she could recall was that first time they were together. Since then, she'd had

Nathan to deal with, Lincoln's kidnapping, and his rejection of her once he found out about Lily. Then there'd been her own kidnapping, and that made dates and other important facts a little blurry in her head. She couldn't remember what month he'd come back into her life, or exactly what day they'd first had sex again, without protection.

She'd gone back through text messages and everything else, but none of it added up to exactly when she got pregnant. It could be three or four months, and June had said it could be four when she did the ultrasound on Roxie. The baby was either four months old or a big three-month-old. Roxie had no clue.

Which would sound stupid when she explained it to the Ob/Gyn down here, but she wouldn't know about the last few months of Roxie's life. It wasn't until she sat down and thought about it all, tried to pin down a conception date, that she realized exactly how much shit she'd been through in such a short period.

But perhaps Lincoln had realized and knew a therapist was the best answer for helping her to get through it all. He should probably see one too, she thought, but wouldn't push. That was something a person had to decide for themself, and Roxie knew that she needed to do this for her child, and the one about to be born. And maybe for the sake of the relationship she would have with Lincoln, romantic or not.

16

Roxie

$\mathcal{A}$ month passed peacefully, with Roxie going to therapy three times a week at first, and then once a week for the past two weeks. Lincoln always took her to every session, picked her up, and when she needed some peace and quiet he'd take her back home, to the beach behind his house, to walk on her own. Sometimes she wanted company and he'd take the whole family out to a restaurant where Lily could play with other kids on the playgrounds while they waited for their food.

She wasn't miraculously cured of her trauma, but she was on the road to recovery, she could feel it. She could also feel her baby now, in the bulge of her stomach and in small kicks and flutters in her abdomen. And the room that remained locked in Lincoln's house? That wasn't so scary now, even if she made a point not to even look at the door when she walked by it.

Time created distance from her memories, from the awfulness of that night, and life with her daughter created a barrier from that darkness. Life goes on, wasn't that what people said so often? And for Roxie, it did.

Only there was still the question lodged between Lincoln and her of what the future held. At one point, she'd considered a future with him in it. She'd almost thought about home, and babies, with days spent picking out furniture while their nights were spent wrapped up together. Then Nathan happened and the main secret she'd hidden from Lincoln for far too long came out. He'd lost it completely when he found out about Lily and that was understandable.

She'd been able to unpack everything, one thing at a time, in her therapy sessions. Since then, she'd come to grips with the fact that she'd never be Chloe again, even if she was set to start using her legal name for everything else in her life. She even had a new bank account, with her real name, and had her old car changed from a friend's name to her own now. She'd been innovative in finding solutions to life in hiding, but she was finished hiding now.

Everyone she knew would continue to call her Roxie,

but she'd begun an imaginary fusing of her past with her present. She was becoming a whole person whose life was separated by one single event. To an extent, that event had changed her into this new person that she was, but being Roxie now was a choice she made without the fear that forced her to be someone else, and that was the most important part.

Lincoln was there for her in every way she'd allow him to be. The way he'd distanced himself from her when he found out about Lily still stung a great deal and she couldn't bring herself to take down the wall that had come up after he rescued her from Celeste. That pain was still too much to get past for someone who'd endured far too much already.

She remembered something else Marie had said to her before she'd flown off with her husband back to their sanctuary. Technically, the position as head of the family was Marie's, as she was her father's daughter, but she was happy for Matteo to take the position he was groomed for. She didn't want anything to do with it, so she'd gladly let him take on the role.

Roxie realized that's what she was doing with Lincoln. He'd taken on the role as head of their small family. She hated the fact that it was what had happened with Celeste that made her second guess her judgment, but she had a feeling he would have done that anyway. She didn't complain, though she did wish she could be the independent woman she used to be again.

But then, she had to admit in one of her therapy sessions that it was kind of nice letting someone else make decisions for her. With time, she knew that independent streak would come back, her confidence was recovering every day, but she still wasn't ready to fly on her own. Besides, Lincoln didn't seem to mind leading the way.

June came to visit five weeks after Roxie's tragic trip to New York. Roxie took her out to lunch while Lincoln went Christmas shopping with Lily.

"You know they're going to come home with a room full of toys, don't you?" June joked as the waiter brought them both glasses of seltzer water with lemon.

"I do, and I'll have a tough time getting Lincoln to understand he's spoiling her." Roxie sipped at the glass of water, her eyes hidden behind sunglasses. She wore a slightly longer wig today, still blonde, but the air was cold, so she'd chosen the wig with hair that came down to a spot between her shoulders. Her fingers tugged at the bottom of the wig, to make sure it hadn't moved.

"Are you wearing those all the time now?" June asked, without making it obvious what she was talking about.

"Not at home. Lily thinks it's funny that I can change my appearance so much. And she likes to play with them." Roxie stuck a finger under the wig, feeling the hair that was little more than silky stubble underneath it. "I went to a beautician down here, once it was certain that my stitches had healed, and had it all cut to the same length. It'll take forever, but it will grow back."

"It will, honey. How's the baby?" June's eyes were hidden behind sunglasses too, but Roxie could tell her smile was genuine.

"He's fine. Definitely a he. No ambiguity there, at all." Roxie showed June the ultrasound picture and laughed when June saw why the baby had been declared a he.

"Are they sure that's not another arm?" June laughed, but she knew better than Roxie how to read an ultrasound, it was part of her job as a fertility specialist.

"You'd know better than me," Roxie replied, patting her belly. "I'm just the incubator."

"Oh, you're more than that, hush." June waved away the notion with her hand and frowned. "I'm sure Lincoln doesn't think of you that way."

"I don't know how he thinks of me, to be honest. It's not something we talk about anymore." Roxie sat back, not defensively, but to distance herself from the question. "Maybe someday down the line, but right now, we aren't a couple. We're two people who live in the same house because we have a child together. I don't know if it will ever change, even after the new baby."

"I'm sorry, Roxie. I know you care deeply for him.

And he does you. Life sucks sometimes," June pouted, but it wasn't malicious. "I really wanted you two to have your happy ever after."

"I know. It's not happening, though. I think we're both too broken to let it happen," Roxie sighed, although it was the truth.

"I hope not. Have you thought about names?" June changed the subject so fast it nearly made Roxie's head spin.

"Michael. I'm not sure. I keep coming back to Michael." Even saying it made her smile. It just felt like the right name for her son.

"I like it. Traditional, strong, a good name. What does Lincoln think?" June sat back in her chair, a smile still on her face.

"Oh, he wants to name him after Kai and Trevon one minute, and then he wants to name him something with an L in the next, to match him and Lily. And Liam of course, which I kind of agree with. Michael Liam Young works, doesn't it?" Roxie pondered the name and decided she liked it.

"I think that would make Liam and Dad both very happy." June sniffled a little, her emotions getting the best of her. "It's just so touching."

"Well, we can't name him after you, unless we name him John in a nod to you, or something like that, but I'm glad you're pleased with that. I'll tell Lincoln our decision when we get home." Roxie laughed, some of that independent streak coming back to life. Her eyes sparkled brightly behind her sunglasses, but nobody could see. She could feel it, and that made a difference.

"He can't override a pregnant mother's decision, that's what I tell my patients and their partners. The pregnant person gets to decide." June laughed at her own joke and Roxie laughed with her.

"That's a good point. I'm doing all of the hard work here." Roxie picked up her glass and took another sip of her water. Her pants were far too tight, but she'd worn them instead of the maternity pants because she thought they were stretchy enough. That was wrong, but she couldn't change it now. "I hate needing stretchy pants."

"Well, as you know from past experience, that's not going to change anytime soon," June pointed out, but whatever else she might have said was deferred because the waiter was bringing them their chicken Caesar salads.

Roxie was trying not to eat too many fatty foods, as well as walking on the beach every day to maintain her energy, and dancing when she could to keep fit. She had to be very careful on the pole, she was showing now, and her center of gravity wasn't the same, but she still loved to dance when she could.

Later, when Lily was in bed and June had headed off to her hotel, Lincoln brought her a grilled cheese sandwich and a glass of apple juice while she watched a movie in the living room. She hadn't asked for the sandwich or the drink, but he must have known she was feeling hungry again.

"Thanks, that's nice of you," she said gratefully and took the plate. "I didn't even know I was hungry."

"You get this look now, a sort of frown that makes your eyebrows come together when you're hungry," Lincoln explained with an easy smile.

"I hope you aren't making fun of me," she said just before she took a bite of the sandwich, her eyes laughing with him.

"No, not at all. But I have started to wonder if you'll gnaw your own leg off if I don't feed you on schedule," he joked, teasing her good-naturedly.

"I might eat yours if you keep it up," she teased back, and took another bite.

"Take what you like, my lady." He gestured at his hips, but then realized what he'd done and froze.

Roxie looked up at him. He stood there, hands in the pockets of his sweatpants, saying nothing, but her eyes were full of laughter. He'd stepped right into that one. "I don't think you want me to take everything."

"No, there are, um, some off-limits parts," he continued, but the tone had changed and she knew it. She didn't shy away from it though. It was nice to play like this with him again, even if it was a dangerous game.

She took another bite of her sandwich and waited, not saying anything else at all. How far would he let this go? For that matter, how far would she let it go? Something flared to life in his eyes as he looked down at her, something familiar that made her bones melt.

Desire.

But would it just be sex?

Would it even go that far? Roxie had no idea what would happen, but she kind of wanted to know.

"Maybe you should let me go hungry once or twice to find out if I'd become that ravenous," she finally said, slowly, softly.

Over the last few days, her dreams had changed, bringing up memories that she tried to hide from when she woke up because they were memories of her nights with Lincoln. Living so close to him wasn't difficult, but it was becoming a bit of a problem as her body demanded a return to the pleasure he used to give her. It wanted what it used to have and didn't care why it was being denied that satisfaction.

Roxie remembered this from her last pregnancy, with Lily. There'd been no way to satisfy her body's craving back then, Lincoln was out of reach, and she didn't want anyone else. There'd been a few offers of a date from guys she'd met, but those stopped when she started to show. Besides, she always told the guys no.

They weren't Lincoln and she didn't want anyone but him.

She hadn't understood quite what was happening to her back then, but now she knew. She needed a fuck, but she didn't want a fuck. She wanted what she couldn't have. She wanted him to worship her body like he used to.

It would pass after the baby came, she'd be too tired to think about sex then, but right now? Her body was raring to go.

Lincoln stood there, looking down at her, the thoughts behind his eyes hidden. Then he swallowed, smiled at her, and left the room. Not tonight then.

Roxie smiled anyway. No matter what, sex dreams of Lincoln were far better than the nightmares, and much more pleasant than some of the dreams she had. She'd wake up ready to jump his bones and strip his clothes off in the morning, as she had this morning when she'd woken up to find a croissant and a glass of orange juice on her nightstand, with him standing over her, but that would be okay. It was all worth it, just to get through the night and into a new day. And once the baby came, it would all change again anyway. Perhaps it was best to stick to dreams and nothing more until then.

17

Roxie

The next day was pure torment. Lincoln worked from home that morning, something he did often now that he had a daughter and a pregnant ex-girlfriend to look after. Roxie had nothing to do, the house was kept clean by Aunt Katie and the shopping was done by Lincoln or his PA. She didn't even have a lunch date or a job to go to. Lincoln had insisted he'd pay her bills and anything else she needed because he didn't want her to jeopardize her health while she was pregnant.

That, and she needed time to heal from her injuries, mental and physical. She'd agreed because she'd been too tired to argue when they first came back from New York. Now she wanted something to do, anything to escape the scent of the man that seemed to be every-where in the house. The dreams last night had been even more powerful, so real she could have sworn he'd actu-ally been there with her in the bed, when she woke up. Only he wasn't. She'd been alone throughout the vivid dreams that had felt so real.

All of her friends were busy, as she'd discovered after sending out dozens of text messages before 9 am. They all had prior engagements or work. June had taken Lily on a trip that would last through the weekend, a trip to a ski resort on the western side of North Carolina. There was no escaping Lincoln, and she couldn't even make up an excuse to get out of the house that wouldn't see him insisting on going with her.

"For fuck's sake," she mumbled, glaring at her closet. "I need to get away from this house for a little while."

With a grim set to her face, she pulled out a pair of black maternity pants, a long black blouse with a generous panel in the front to accommodate her belly, and the boots Lincoln had bought for her. She was going to go somewhere, alone. Even if she had to insist on it. This was not going to end well if she was stuck around the house all day with him here.

"Where are you off to?" Lincoln asked when she made it downstairs, pulling on her coat as she came down.

"Um, just out. I'm a little stir crazy." She grabbed her

bag from a hook on the wall by the front door, frantically digging around in it for her keys. *Here it comes, I just know he's going to say it.*

And he didn't disappoint her. "Oh, hold on, I'll go with you."

"No!" She shouted without meaning to. She looked around at him, with a wince of apology. "Sorry, no, it's fine. I need to get out. On my own."

"I see," he said, his eyes narrowing. "Are you alright, Roxie?"

"I'm fine," she insisted, forcing a smile on her face. *I'm just going to assault you if I don't leave right now.* "I have some personal things I need to get and I'd like to stretch my legs. You get your work done, I'll be fine."

He didn't like letting her out on her own since that trip to New York and she knew why, he wanted to know she was safe, but she was only going to the mall. It wasn't that far away. And he'd let June take Lily hours away, which had surprised Roxie, but she'd agreed to the trip too. They all needed to get back to life and right now, Roxie needed some privacy, even if it was in one of the most public places you could be. She needed some time away from him more than anything.

She couldn't think rationally when he was so close. Her brain insisted on remembering things like how his skin felt beneath her fingers, what it felt like to have him in her mouth, inside her body. And the sounds he made when she moved in time with him, fuck, those soft groans and moans had haunted her all night. Even now, the memory was there, making her cheeks hot and her knees a little wobbly.

Lincoln stared at her, watching her for signs of distress. Roxie tried to school her features, tried to keep her face calm, and he must have bought it because he nodded in agreement. "Okay. Just keep your phone on please, and buzz me if you need me for anything, alright?"

Roxie nodded energetically, eager to get away now that he'd finally agreed to what she needed the most. "I'll only be a couple of hours, maybe. If I'm going to be longer, I'll let you know."

"Thanks. Have fun."

Roxie waved and got out through the door as quickly as she could. Her small SUV started up right away, and she was at the nearest mall in less than ten minutes. It was wintertime and early in the morning still. Traffic was light and she was at the entrance to the mall, looking around trying to decide where to go first, now that she was free.

That made her smile. Living with Lincoln wasn't so bad, she was just feeling cloistered, and far too aroused to be in that house for one more second. The first thing she did was get some breakfast, giving in to the craving for a sausage biscuit that she washed down with some orange juice. Then she headed to a shop that was strictly for maternity clothes. She had a credit card with her that Lincoln had told her to use as she wished. And today, she wished for new dresses that weren't too tight. There were a few tops she wanted as well, and then she found herself in the lingerie section of the shop. Looking around, Roxie found some maternity nightgowns and pajamas that were cute and suitable for most nights at home. But it was the black silk nightgown and lacy robe that went with it that drew her eyes over and over again.

She decided to try one on, not because she had a plan or anything, but because for the first time in a long time, she wanted to feel sexy again. With the permission of a saleswoman, Roxie went into a booth to try the outfit on. The white cubicle had mirrors on all four sides, and Roxie had a good view from every angle, once she'd managed to get into the nightgown and robe.

The nightgown was a basic slip shape with triangular cups at the top with underwires to support her heavy breasts. The material was gathered below her bust, with a lot of material to cover her belly. The lace robe was a perfect compliment that went down to her knees and sheer enough that nothing was left to the imagination.

Lincoln's jaw would hit the floor if she came out wearing this for dinner tonight, she thought with a smirk of delight. Not that she would do that, but if she did…

Fantasies blossomed in her mind. Filthy, dirty fantasies that left her feeling flush. Getting out of the robe and gown quickly, Roxie dressed, exited the booth, and stared at the pile of clothes she'd left at the counter already. She'd intended to put the sexy lingerie back but found herself watching as the saleswoman folded it up and put it in a box.

Then, she found herself paying for it all and leaving the store.

She would not wear it, she kept telling herself, it was just there for those nights when she felt fat and ungainly. That was all.

Roxie did a little more shopping, adding some shoes that felt alright on her toes to the pile of bags she already had, and a few gifts for Lily, Lincoln, and Aunt Katie for Christmas. When she left the store, she felt a little triumphant. For the longest time, she'd been afraid to go out on her own. Lincoln took her everywhere she needed to go so it hadn't been an issue really. She hadn't had to face that fear, not until being too close to him nearly drove her insane with need.

Okay, so she hadn't solved world hunger, and she hadn't won a marathon, but this small victory was just that, a victory over her own fears. Now if only she could conquer this feeling that she'd been hypnotized by him every time she was near him, she might come out of this alright. Getting back in her car, she drove herself back to the house, only to find it empty.

Lincoln had left a note saying he needed to go out but he'd be back shortly. Roxie took it as an opportunity to try her new clothes on properly. The dresses were fine, long-sleeved, gathered under the bust, the same pattern, just different colors with one black and the other emerald green. The tops fit fine and would be good for everyday wear. Roxie put them away, along with the pairs of boots and sneakers that she'd bought, leaving the bag with the nightgown in it. Roxie took the lid off the box and looked down at it with a smile.

Lincoln was out, she was alone, why not?

Roxie put the nightgown on first, comfortable because Lincoln kept the house warm. She adjusted the straps until everything was just right and then put the robe on. Looking at herself in the floor-length mirror, she decided to take the long blonde wig off and looked at her image. Even with the super-short hair, she didn't look bad. Turning to the side to look at her profile, Roxie smiled again. Even with her belly poking out, she still didn't look bad. Not bad at all.

Her right hand moved from her belly up to her hair. She kind of liked the look, even if she hadn't made the choice to cut it so short. The bruises under her eyes and the cuts on her lips were gone, all that remained now was a woman who'd been through hell but still stood on her own two feet.

Going to the bed, Roxie sat down with her eyes still on the image in the mirror. She'd overcome everything that had been thrown her way. Her parents would be proud of her. Maybe she hadn't ended up the kind of dancer they had hoped for, and she'd never been to Paris, but she had survived. She'd lived through all of it and that was enough.

Going to New York on her own had been stupid, but in the end, Celeste had been dealt with, as had the two men who'd killed her parents. Because of her, Marie could now live in the open without fear of being killed by a woman who had it in for her. Because of her decision, she could live out in the open now.

That was a new perspective on it all, one that brought tears to her eyes. She'd taken her fate in her own hands, and she'd nearly lost. For too long she'd sat in this house, second-guessing every decision that she had to make. She'd deferred to Lincoln, trusting him to make the decisions. Which wasn't wrong, but she'd allowed herself to become…nothing. That wouldn't work, not at all.

Her pride came back to life as she looked at herself in the mirror, even with the tears streaming down her face. Or maybe because of the tears streaming down her face, she decided, getting up to look at herself more closely. She was used to living her life, telling people to fuck off if they didn't like how she decided to live that life, and doing exactly as she damn well pleased.

For a while, she'd allowed herself to lose sight of that, but now she saw that fire burning again in her eyes. She saw determination, which had been dormant for too long.

"Are you alright, Roxie?" Lincoln's voice came through the door just before he pushed it open.

Roxie turned around, about to tell him not to come in, but it was too late. His jaw hung open and his eyes were moving up and down her, taking in the sight of her body. "Um, yeah, I'm fine."

"You are, indeed." He didn't look away, or turn around, he just openly stared with hungry eyes going over her again and again. He leaned into the doorway, his hands in the pockets of the charcoal gray trousers he had on. "You look very good, actually."

Roxie's breath caught in her throat and she looked away. This hadn't been part of the plan, but she wanted him. She'd always wanted him, even when she'd hated him as a teenager. "I'm sorry, I thought you'd be gone longer. I'll change."

"No, don't," he said quickly, holding his hand out. "Please, don't."

"But, Lincoln?" She made the two words a question.

She wasn't sure what she was asking, but he seemed to know.

"Roxie, come here." He twitched his hand, refusing to budge. He wanted her to come to him.

Roxie stared at his hand, knowing she shouldn't go near him, but she couldn't say no. Not anymore. He was what she wanted, what she'd missed, what she needed, and she couldn't deny it anymore. Her feet moved before she'd told them to, taking her to him.

Warmth flowed from his hand and up her arm as she placed her hand in his. Blue eyes crashed into brown, and she forgot what she might have wanted to say. But Lincoln hadn't.

"It's been too long, Roxie. I've wanted to tell you for weeks now that I made a mistake, that I'd been incredibly stupid. And honestly, I think I was stupid all those years ago when I left you in the hotel room alone. I should have stayed with you, I should have told you then that you were the only woman I'd ever love."

"What?" She asked, shocked at what he'd admitted.

"I've loved you since you were fourteen years old, Roxie. Remember that first time you told me to fuck off? You made me laugh but I also knew you meant it. You were so fierce, strong, sure of what you wanted." He ran a finger down her cheek to her jaw, but his eyes stayed on hers. "And when I found you as an adult, this larger-than-life dancer with eyes full of fire and damnation, fuck, I didn't think it was possible to love you more, but every single day, you prove me wrong."

"You love me, Lincoln?" Roxie could have rolled her eyes at the stupid question, but it wasn't so stupid. She'd given him the biggest reason in the world to hate her. "But, I kept Lily from you."

"Yes, but you did it to protect her. I understand that now. You did what you thought was best when you were the one left to make huge decisions on your own. You didn't do it to be malicious. I was a dick about it when I found out, and I'm sorry for that. I wish I could change it, but I can't. I can only try to learn from that mistake and not repeat it. If you'll let me, I'd like to spend the rest of my life proving to you how sorry I am, Roxie." He paused, moved his hand to his pocket, and pulled out a ring that made her eyes nearly pop.

"Lincoln?" Her brain was stuck on making her sound stupid, but she didn't pull her hand back because she wanted this. She hadn't realized how much she'd wanted this. "But we're supposed to be the ones who snub their noses at convention."

"Fuck that. Fuck conventions, fuck what we're supposed to be, Roxie. Let's just be us, and do whatever the fuck we want to, shall we? And what I want, what I'd really love, is for you to be my wife." His eyes pleaded for an answer.

She moved her fingers, holding her ring finger up to

him. She wanted to pull it back as soon as she saw her bare nail beds, but he clutched at her hand.

"I need to hear you say it, Rox," he said, holding the ring just out of reach of her finger.

"Hear what, Lincoln?" Her eyes were on his again, full of tears. This wasn't a dream. It was real. It was happening.

"Say you'll marry me. Say you forgive me. Say you love me." His eyes implored her to do his bidding.

18

Roxie

"Yes, I'll marry you, Lincoln. Yes, I forgive you. But most of all? Yes, I do love you."

She sniffled on a sob, holding her other hand up to her mouth as he slid the giant diamond on her finger.

She was in his arms the moment the ring was on, crushed against his chest as he made a sound above her that she could comprehend. It could have been relief, joy, she didn't know but didn't mind either way. She had what she hadn't let herself dare to wish for. A promise from him that he'd always be hers.

The walls crumbled down, the fear faded away, everything disappeared when Lincoln tilted her face up to his and kissed her with so much intensity, she thought she'd collapse.

Roxie tore at the buttons of his shirt, finally settling for just ripping the panels apart when her fingers didn't want to work. The tips were still sensitive to things like buttons and she was impatient. Desire had flared into bright burning life the second his lips touched hers and she didn't want to wait to feel his bare chest or to slide her hands up to his shoulders.

It didn't matter anymore what had happened in the past, it was time for the new now. New memories, new moments, new hope.

Lincoln lifted his mouth from hers and pulled back to look at her. "Are you sure?"

"About marrying you? Definitely. About this? About touching you?" She paused, biting her lip as she slid her right hand up to cup his face. "I've never been more sure, Lincoln."

His breath hissed in between his teeth and his eyes went wide. "Good, because I don't think I could have spent another night alone. I've missed you so much."

"I've needed that time alone, but I have to say, Lincoln. I've missed you terribly." There was nothing between their chests now, except a scrap of silk that did little to hold back the heat coming off his skin.

"Prove it," he said with a teasing smirk. He pulled

away from her, holding out his hand as he did so. "Prove to me how much you've missed me."

Roxie gave him the dirtiest smile she could muster and followed.

Lincoln kicked off his shoes before he climbed into her bed and relaxed against her pillows. It wasn't even lunchtime yet, but it didn't matter to either of them as Roxie followed the man she'd loved, even when she didn't know it was love that she felt for him. The new ring on her finger would take some getting used to, but she didn't mind its presence when she climbed over him, settling on top of him, his hips pressed into hers.

"Like this, Lincoln? Is this how you want me to prove it?" She asked, her right hand on his flat stomach. Her eyes traveled up the hard muscles in his abdomen and up to his eyes.

"Just like that, darlin'," he answered, his right hand coming up to her hip, to hold her in place while he thrust up into her. "Just like that."

Her thighs tensed around him as she pushed down against him, loving the familiar feel of him there. Where he'd always belonged.

Roxie leaned forward, needing to feel Lincoln's warmth. Her skin felt ice-cold against the fire in Lincoln's skin. The contrast of sensitive, silky skin against the rough scrape of Lincoln's open shirt distracted Roxie and for a breathtaking second, she felt completely over-whelmed. But it wasn't a bad thing, Lincoln's mouth consumed hers again, taking everything she dared to give.

She was aware that his right hand moved, that it slid down the silky front panel of her gown, over the bulge of her stomach, and down, further, until she felt the tip of his finger sliding into her aching walls.

"Lincoln," Roxie breathed his name against his lips, pleasure making it hard to think beyond his name.

"Just let me feel you, baby," Lincoln murmured against her lips, his fingers tracing down her jaw when her head moved to the pillow, her lips opening to take his finger between her teeth.

Roxie moaned around his finger, loving the images that popped into her head when she gently bit down on it and simply loving how good it felt to have something in her mouth as his fingers slid deeper inside of her, opening her for much more later. She made him moan when she sucked on the finger in her mouth, a promise of what could be if he wanted it.

She nearly protested when he removed the finger between her teeth to slide it down to the curve of her breast. The tip of his index finger teased at the swell of her nipple, making her forget all about where that finger had been seconds before. Lincoln breathed a moan of delight when Roxie's back arched, pushing her breast into his hand for more.

"I want to touch your skin, but I love this material. It feels so nice, touching you through it." Lincoln pushed her up gently, just enough to bring the globes up to his face.

Roxie hovered over him, anticipating the sensation of his tongue touching her through the silk. The cloth turned cold as his tongue lapped at her nipple, wetting the black silk until it clung to the taut peak, a new sensation she hadn't expected at all. Then his teeth locked gently around the bud just as his palm rocked into one of the most sensitive spots on her body.

"Oh," she breathed the sigh out long and deep, giving herself up to everything he made her feel.

"You respond to the slightest touch. It's always fascinated me, how receptive you are. I've watched you so many times, the way you touch yourself, watching how you like to be touched. I've watched you so often lately, wanting to touch you, but I knew I couldn't." His thumb and forefinger gripped at her nipple softly, teasing it until her hips ground down into him as he whispered the words to her, even though they were completely alone. Her eyes were caught by his, watching the way he watched her as he brought her body to life.

"I keep thinking about the way your body moved when I touched you, the way your face would change when I made you come. I've missed the way your back arches when I slide into you. I've desperately missed being inside of you, fucking you as your body closed around me, taking me deeper into you. Fuck, I've missed everything about you."

Holy moly, he was going to get her off before she even got his pants off, she thought, as his lips teased at her other nipple through her gown. She pressed her breast into his face, wanting more, loving the sensation of the silky swipe of his tongue through the cloth, but she wanted so much more.

"Lincoln, give me more," she pleaded, rocking her hips, pushing against Lincoln's hand, clutching at his shoulders to support her torso as she focused on one thing: feeling the intense pleasure he was giving her.

"Are you ready for me, Roxie? Or do you want me to finish you off like this?" He asked, focusing on her eyes as she stared down at him.

She went still for a moment, thinking. She didn't want to wait, but she also wanted him inside of her. And if he was inside of her, oh it would be so good.

"Oh yes, fuck me, please. I need you inside of me more than I need anything else, right now." She'd made them both wait far too long, and they might just combust once he was finally where he belonged, but she didn't care. She wanted him and didn't care what it cost them.

Lincoln pushed at her with his hips until she figured

out she needed to move. He couldn't get his pants off with her on top of him.

"Be careful," Lincoln warned her as she moved off of him, supporting her as much as he could. Lincoln stood up, pushing his pants off and tearing his shirt away from his arms. He crawled back onto the bed, watching her like a lion watches a gazelle.

"What?" She asked, confused by the way he was looking at her.

"How is this going to be best for you?" He asked finally, still on his hands and knees.

"Probably like that," she answered, without thinking.

"Taking it from behind always was one of your favorite positions," Lincoln said with a cheeky grin.

"Well, yes, it is, but like this," she pointed at her stomach, "it's probably the easiest way. I don't know. I've never had sex while pregnant. Maybe we should try out every position?"

She leaned back against the pillows and smiled over at him, a dare in her eyes.

"Then every position it is, my lady," he chuckled softly, but then his eyes changed, and the intensity from before came right back.

His head dipped, swiping a long lick between her folds before he moved back up her body to kiss her. He knew she loved tasting herself on his tongue, on his face. "Do you want me to get a condom?"

"No, why? I'm already pregnant." She grinned, enjoying the joke.

"I thought it would be best to ask, that's all." His rueful smile told her he'd got the joke. Her belly wasn't huge yet so he could still lean over her to kiss her deep and hard. Her hands came up to grasp at his face, to hold his mouth there with hers.

He slid into her then, when she was caught up in his kiss, surprising her into gasping into his mouth.

"Lincoln. Fuck. You feel so good."

Lincoln pushed in deeper, opening her inch by inch until she had all of him she could take.

"Fuck, I forgot how tight you are!" Lincoln gasped, his eyes closed in ecstasy.

Instead of answering him, Roxie moved her hips, trying to get him to move inside of her, but it seemed he was enjoying simply being in her too much.

Lincoln moved a hand between them, searching for and finding that sensitive spot that made her gasp before he began to move inside of her.

"Just, fuck, don't stop!" Roxie cried as her body exploded, gripping at Lincoln, pulsing around him like she never wanted to let him go. It had been too long, she hadn't even got herself off since that night, and he was just too good at getting her off. She stopped caring about anything, about what she should do, what she wanted to do, and just became light wrapped in erotic pleasure. She rode the waves that pulsed through her, listening to him gasp as she moved against him, her heels digging into the bed as her back arched, pushing her down onto him, nearly dragging him with her into the nothingness.

Roxie could only sigh when the pressure of his finger between her legs became too much and she had to twitch her hips and hold his hand still with her own. It had been good, but it was too much now. Lincoln could play games, force her right into another orgasm, but he was being gentle with her.

She wasn't ready for those kinds of games just yet, and thankfully, he knew it. "I love you, Lincoln."

The words came out of nowhere, a need that formed so suddenly she couldn't stop her voice from speaking them. She had to tell him, so she did.

"I love you, Roxie," he answered, staring into her eyes. "But I can't wait any longer. I need to finish."

"Then finish, baby," she answered, relaxing so that he'd know everything was okay. "You'll take me with you."

"I will," he promised, just before he moved her hips, tilting her up a little, as he drove down into her, striving for the right spot. As she knew it would, each thrust drove new pleasure into her, until she felt her back arch, her heels once again digging into the bed as she matched his pace.

Lincoln thrust harder with her, into just the right spot, a spot that started the quaking inside of her all over again. She couldn't breathe, her lungs were so tight, and air was hard to gasp in, but it didn't matter, not when it felt so good.

Lincoln watched her, drinking in the sight of her face as she watched him, the way his body moved with hers, until she heard him gasp and go still. "Come on baby, take me with you."

"Fuck, Roxie. Don't stop," he gasped when she reached for his nipples and twisted them intensely. It was a pleasurable pain, a pain that he liked, and she was willing to give it to him because it only made him thrust deeper, faster, taking her with him, as she'd asked him to.

His head fell back when he finally let himself go, gasping every time she clenched around him. Together their bodies pulsed around and within each other, taking and giving all that they could. At last, they were one, and there was nothing that could tear them apart ever again. Not anymore.

Roxie smiled at him when he withdrew from her and nestled up beside her. "I hope you don't think we're done."

"As if," he answered, pulling her into his arms. "I'll never get enough of you, anyway. Ever."

"Good, because I'm not letting you go ever again."

She cuddled into his chest, her hand over his heart. This was home, right here with him, where nothing could ever get to her.

Soon they'd have another child that they'd raise together, along with the daughter that he'd missed so much time with. They had it all now, together.

"I still hate you, though, even if I do love you," she teased and heard his laughter rumble under her ear.

"Good. I love you too, princess."

19

Roxie

One Year Later

"Michael and Lily are with June, Aunt Katie is going to the movies, and I'm dressed and ready to go. Are you on your way home?" Roxie asked, holding the phone up to her face as she brushed her hair out. It was down to her shoulders now, her real hair, blonde as always without any dye in it at all. It would have been longer, but she'd had it cut not long ago.

There were no signs now of her former injuries, and even her nails were coated in gel polish with a black and gold design on them. A pair of heels pinched at her toes, the only pain she felt in them now. And her waist had recovered from pregnancy, although she was a little thicker now than she had been before Michael's conception. She didn't mind, and Lincoln certainly didn't complain, so she didn't force herself into an exercise regimen that would melt the pounds away. She just enjoyed being Mom to a new baby and his sister.

"I'm going in the suit I have on, so I'll just drive up if you don't mind?" He asked over the phone's speaker, and Roxie could hear the sounds of traffic. He was driving with the windows down again even though it was winter, silly man. "Oh, hey, could you get my cufflinks out of my jewelry box?"

"Sure, the onyx ones?" She moved over to the box, digging around looking for the cufflinks. A shelf moved inside the box, a tiny velvet shelf that held rings, revealing the edge of a piece of paper. Curious, she moved the shelf more, frowning when she saw the shape of the paper. It looked like one of the love notes she used to exchange with his brother.

"Yeah, those. I have the titanium ones on at the moment, but I like the onyx better. Did you find them?"

"Not yet," she drew out the last word, her thoughts focused on the letter. She turned it over in her hand and recognized the writing on the fold that tucked underneath another fold. She'd learned to fold the letters into packets online, a skill shared by countless teenagers in previous generations that was probably lost on kids now.

She frowned, despite the urge to smile. What was Lincoln doing with one of her letters to Liam? She pulled the other little shelves and boxes out and found six more letters. He had so many of them. How?

"Lincoln?" She said as a question, more of a warning.

"What babe?" He asked, obviously distracted with driving.

"Nothing, nothing." She spotted the cufflinks in one of the shelves, grabbed them along with the letters, and put them all in a little handbag she would be taking with her. "Found your cufflinks. Shall I meet you outside?"

"Sure, I'll be there in five," he answered, completely clueless to the trouble he was about to come home to.

She had on a long, blue dress that matched her eyes, but she wore a long black coat over it, to protect her from the cold. On her left hand, a diamond gleamed in the moonlight, matching the twinkling from the watch on her wrist. It had been her mother's watch, a watch she'd given to him to pay for a loan he gave her a lifetime ago. He'd given it back to her just before Michael was born, knowing she'd like to have it.

In the last year, she'd finally reclaimed her old identity, claimed her inheritance, which was nothing to sneeze at, and was now kept in trust for her children, and she'd given birth to their son. She'd also been working on opening a new club with her friends and their husbands. It wasn't Elmo's, it was much better.

Tonight was the grand opening, and they were going to be late if he didn't hurry up and get here. She heard the sound of his car and looked up, a gleam in her eyes. She was going to find out exactly why he had Liam's letters from her, one way or another.

Because over the last year she'd got her confidence back, along with the independent streak she'd thought was long gone. Lincoln had helped her with that, allowed her to grow into who she was now, encouraged her to reach for her dreams and do what she wanted to do. He was an investor in her club, proving just how much he believed in her. But he had something he shouldn't have, and she wanted to know why and how.

"Hi babe," he said as soon as she got in the car.

"Hi, honey, here's your cufflinks." She handed them over to him, knowing he'd want to put them on right away. He took off the ones he had and handed them over so she could put them in her bag.

"Thanks, you're an angel." He leaned over to kiss her before he put the car in reverse to pull out of the driveway.

"I also found these," she said, and pulled out the letters. "How did you get these, Lincoln?"

"What? Ohhhh." He looked at the letters and

blanched before he looked at her. Luckily, he hadn't pulled out just yet. "Those."

His face was a mask of guilt as his eyes came up to hers, worried.

"Yes, these. They were to your brother. Why do you have them?" She looked at him with a glare, not backing down, but not being hateful. She just wanted answers.

"Well, you see, um." Lincoln frowned, put the car in park, and turned to face her. "I had to borrow Liam's biology book one day and found the letter tucked into it. I asked him about it, and he said he wasn't that interested in you. But, um, I was. Very."

"Okay. But he wrote me back." Her left eyebrow lifted, warning that he was in danger. "*He* wrote me back, right Lincoln?"

"Ummmm." His cheeks turned red, very red, and his lips pursed until they almost disappeared. "Well, you see, Rox…"

"Yes?" She asked with a snip, starting to see the truth, even if he couldn't bring himself to say it yet.

"I wrote you back. I decided to write the first one on a whim. Then I planned to tell you, but you seemed so into him and, well, shit." He paused, running his right hand through his hair, his frown growing deeper. "I wanted you to like me so much, but after a while, I couldn't figure out how to tell you it was me. I kept watching you watching him, and I felt like such a dick. I just didn't know how to fix it, and then everything happened."

He held his hands out, at a loss now.

"So, you wrote me those letters that touched me so much, that made my little teenage heart melt like butter?" She asked, pretending to be angry.

"Yeah, it was me. I'm sorry, really. I just wanted some small part of you, to matter to you, and well, it wasn't a good thing to do, but I really liked you, Roxie. I loved you."

"I'm kind of glad it was you, after all, Lincoln," she said, after a pause where she looked out the window, thinking of all the things he'd promised her, and he'd kept every one so far. It took a little while, but he'd given her far more than she could have dreamed of. When she spoke, she turned her head back to him, a wide smile on her face.

"What?" He breathed out in relief.

"I'm glad it was you and not Liam. I don't think he could have made me as happy as you do every day, Lincoln. And you kept the letters! That's so sweet." She leaned over to kiss him softly before she fell back. "All is forgiven."

"Phew." He wiped at his brow and put the car in drive. "I'm kind of glad you know now. I've carried those around with me all over the world, even though they weren't to me. I hoped one day, they would be to me."

"I'll write you dozens, Lincoln. And a few more just to be sure." She promised as he drove them along.

"That would be nice. Maybe a little dirtier would be nicer?" He prompted. "Wait, didn't you mention a kiss in those letters?"

"Oh. Yes. There were a couple, but then he just stopped for some reason." Roxie was the one with hot cheeks now.

"I bet that's when he was dating Sara. She was this girl who was already out of high school, she finished the year before he did. He had a big thing for her, but she wasn't interested enough to make it work." Lincoln revealed something Roxie hadn't known before.

"Maybe so. Anyway, he lost his chance. Lucky us." She put her hand over his on the gear shift for a moment before she took it away.

"Yes, very lucky us. Do I turn left here or right?" He asked and Roxie pointed to the left.

"It's just over there." Roxie pointed, even though he'd been here dozens of times. He could never remember which way to turn at the intersection, for some reason.

It was a four-story building, all glass on the front, but opaque so nobody could see inside. Lincoln pulled up to the front, helped her out of the car, and then gave the keys to the valet who would park it.

"Okay, on this floor is the dance club and the adult

club," Roxie said, giving him the tour as the doors opened as soon as she walked up with him. "I know we were going to put the adult club upstairs, but we decided to keep it down here."

She'd worked hard to find the right building and get everything done with all of her friends helping along the way. It was a group effort, and group-funded, so she'd done her very best to create a fantasy that was also worth paying money to visit. "The restaurant is on this floor too."

"Okay. And the private dancing areas?" Lincoln asked softly. Only certain members would be allowed above the first floor and not everyone would know what was up there, no matter how curious they might be. Those floors were strictly for exclusive members who paid the fees to get up there.

"Upstairs too." Roxie wrapped her arms around Lincoln's right arm as they walked in and found a group ready to greet them. Someone handed her champagne and Roxie took it.

"This place is awesome," River, a former protégé, said with a grin. "I can't wait to get to work here."

"You and Kitty will be busy, that's for sure," Emily, a dear friend and former co-worker with her own hidden story, said with a smile of delight. "It's beautiful, Roxie. I love it."

"Thanks, Emily."

"Can I get a job up here, Rox? I might need a new career," Wendy asked as she came up behind her friend.

"Any time, honey. But wait until after the wedding, won't you? I don't need one of my bridesmaids calling off because she can't get off of work."

"Sure, honey." Wendy hugged her with a laugh and glanced around. "You have ten minutes left before the crowd's allowed in, right?"

"Yeah, they've all been herded into the restaurant for now. I just wanted to thank you all for investing in the club, for believing in me, and helping me get this far before we open up to the public. So, here's to all of you, and thank you." Roxie held up her champagne glass as she toasted all the faces around her.

There were more people than she thought there'd be, but that was fine. Everyone had helped in some way, with money or time, and she was grateful to them all. Keily was here with her husband Logan, some of Emily's brothers were here too, having invested in the venture after Emily sold them on the idea. Their names wouldn't be attached to any documents, but there was definitely Thompson money in this little experiment of hers.

"Here's to you, Roxie. You've been through hell and come out of it a queen. You have my deepest, lifelong respect and love, baby. Good luck, but I know you won't need it." Lincoln held his own glass up as he toasted her, making Roxie's eyes sparkle with tears of happiness.

"Thank you, baby," she said and took a deep breath. "Let's just hope our wedding this summer is as easy to pull off."

Everyone laughed at that and Roxie was finally able to wander off, to watch as the clients were finally allowed into the adult club section of the building. She saw men and women, alone and as couples or groups, walking in, looking around in amazement.

The place was decorated with a lot of black glass and gold accents all over. It wasn't gaudy, it was tasteful, with a stage at one end, a bar at the other, and black tile floors throughout.

"Congratulations," Lincoln said as he came up beside her, whispering into her ear with a seductive brush of his lips. "Do we have a room upstairs? I just remembered watching you dance, and I'd like a private performance."

"Anytime, my love, you know that." She turned into his arms, ready for wherever he might lead them.

"I do, but I wanted to be sure. Show me the way, Roxie. You know I'll follow wherever you lead."

"Just as I'll follow you, Lincoln. I love you," she whispered the words against his lips, loving how much he still turned her on, even after another baby, and time, should have dulled their passion.

She had a feeling that was never going to change. They were fire together, and always would be. And as long as they continued to lead each other through their lives together, she knew that would never change. She took his hand behind her back and started to walk out of the club to the elevators. It was time to start the next adventure with him.

20

Epilogue

Lincoln

"He's here, Lincoln. Are you sure about this?" Roxie asked, staring steadily at the man who would be her husband in a week.

"Yes, my love. Let him in." Lincoln stood up in his office, brushing down his shirt and straightening his tie. This was an important meeting, not a business one, but very personal. He didn't want to impress the man who was about to walk into his office, he wanted the man to know he was fine without him, actually. But he did want to meet him.

"Hi," the older man said as he came into the room, looking around nervously. "I'm Colin Fuller. Your dad."

"Hi," Lincoln said and looked the man over. He was in his fifties, but his head was bald, his face lined with stress and too much sun. He looked much older than he was.

Lincoln knew a lot more about the man than he knew about Lincoln, he was certain of that. Lincoln had him investigated and knew Colin had a record, that he'd caused a terrible accident a few years after Lincoln's mother left him. He'd turned his life around after that, started a construction business, and had become mildly successful from it. He was involved in a lot of youth outreach programs now and spent a lot of time trying to make up for the pain he'd caused to the other driver of the car he'd hit while drunk.

Colin brushed his hands along the seat of his blue jeans and held his hand out. Lincoln took it, accepting the man into his life. For now.

"I don't want anything from you, I just thought we should meet. If you want to walk out of here and never come back, that's fine," Lincoln offered, showing the man to a seat that he took.

"No, I couldn't forgive myself if I walked out of your life a second time." The man's lips pursed, shame crossing his features. "I'm not who I was then. I have a wife, two other boys, and a daughter too. I've been with them every day since I married Sheryl. I've wondered what happened to you, but, well, your mother made it clear I wasn't going to be a part of your life."

"No, I'm sure she wouldn't have allowed it with the way things were going. Yes, she told me the truth." Lincoln paused, trying to come to terms with what his mother had told him and the man now before him. "I've had you investigated. I know what you've done, how you've tried to change who you were."

"I have. It was the right thing to do after that accident I caused. I nearly killed that poor man," Colin replied, and Lincoln could see that even now, his father felt the guilt. "Your mother took you away, right after you were born. It was probably for the best. I wasn't a good person to be around. I don't know what she told you, but I was terrible to her. Absolutely terrible."

"Everything. She told me all of it. Do you still drink?" Lincoln offered him a bottle of very expensive scotch but Colin shook his head and held up his hand.

"No. Thank you, but no. I don't touch the stuff anymore. I haven't in over twenty years." Colin looked around the room, but not with greed. He was just looking around. "You've done well for yourself. I'm glad to see that."

"Thanks. I have. My soon-to-be wife is doing pretty well for herself, too." Lincoln sat down after grabbing two bottles of water from a mini-fridge. He handed one to his father and took the other to his desk. "I'd like to ask you and your family to my wedding. I'd like to meet my siblings, if that would be alright with you. If you don't like that idea, it's fine too."

"No, I've told them all about you, even before your attorney contacted me. I told them all they had an older brother out there somewhere. And I told them why they didn't know him, as well. I knew when they were born, I had to be honest with them, that all of my preaching about clean living and being a good person would just wash over them if I didn't give them a reason as to why I'd changed my ways. They know everything."

"Alright. Then, I'd like to meet them. And your wife." Lincoln watched Colin and saw when the man smiled. Good, there was no subterfuge there. The guy was being honest.

"They'd love that." Colin nodded, as if to emphasize the statement. "They've always wondered about you. And they're all hard workers too."

Colin said that last part suddenly, as if to stave off any worries Lincoln might have about his siblings asking for money.

"The oldest, Mark, he's a foreman at my company, and John went to college. He's in medical school now. And Janey, my daughter, she's in the Navy. Loves it." Colin smiled with pride for his other children and then looked up to give Lincoln a steady look. "I wish I could have been the kind of man your mother deserved, but at that point, I was barely human. I couldn't be the father you deserved either, and I'm sorry about that, Lincoln. I really am."

"I'm fine, really. My mother married quite often, but I had a father figure I could depend on, even after she divorced him. He's still a part of my life, and will be at the wedding too." Lincoln didn't know what else to say. He'd known this would probably be awkward, he'd talked about it with Roxie, and she'd told him if he ran out of things to say to call her and the kids in. He decided to do that now. She'd told him that kids level everything out, put people on equal footing at the whim of children. "Would you like to meet your grandchildren?"

"You have children?" Colin looked up in wonder, his eyes full of delight.

"I do. Michael was born in the spring and Lily turned ten this year." Lincoln smiled with his own paternal pride. "Their mother and I had a thing when we were younger and got back together after we were separated for a long time."

Lincoln didn't want to go into the full story right now, but he'd tell the man, eventually, if it got that far. It was Roxie's story too, and he wouldn't tell it without her permission. Lincoln got up and walked to the door. "Roxie?"

"Yes, babe?" She asked, coming out of the living room. "Want the kids?"

Her smile was everything he needed in that moment. Reassuring, full of love, and overflowing with kindness. "Yes, please."

"Okay, be there in five." Roxie went up to get the kids from Aunt Katie and was back in just a few minutes. "This is Lily, say hello to Mr. Fuller, and this little bundle of joy is Michael."

Roxie kept Michael in her arms as Colin looked him over and shook his granddaughter's hand. Lily hid behind Lincoln's chair, her hand on his, once she'd shaken Colin's hand, but she soon came out to smile at the stranger.

"Would you like something to eat, Colin?" Roxie asked, rocking Michael gently to keep him quiet while she talked.

"No, no thank you. I had a burger on the way here." Colin smiled politely at Roxie and looked at Michael again. He wasn't ignoring Lily, it was just that the girl was stuck to her father's side and didn't want to budge.

Lincoln watched the man's eyes as he looked at Michael, surprised when he saw tears of joy in his eyes. "He's beautiful."

"Thank you," Roxie answered with her own pride, looking over at Lincoln. Lincoln nodded at her, letting her know all was well. "He and his sister are our pride and joy. Aren't you Lily?"

"Yes, Mommy," Lily answered automatically, all the fingers of her left hand around Lincoln's fingers. She wasn't frightened, just shy. Lincoln had done this with her dozens of times, always determined to be her protector, even if she had no reason to be afraid. He wouldn't force her to hug the stranger or kiss him, she'd do that in her own time, if she chose to. "Are you like Papa George?"

"Who?" Colin asked, looking over at Roxie for an answer.

"That's Lincoln's former stepfather and his sister's father. He's still a part of Lincoln's life. Lily calls him Papa George." Roxie provided the information with a smile.

"Your mother had another child?" Colin asked, surprised.

"Yes, my sister June. She's a doctor," Lincoln answered with a nod. "Her father is a doctor, as is her half-brother, so it wasn't a surprise when she went into medicine too."

"Your mother must be very proud of you both." Colin nodded, his eyes bright with humor. "Especially with June being a doctor. Not that you aren't impressive too, I just don't understand what fintech is."

"Not a lot of people do, it's alright," Lincoln

answered, smoothing over the moment that could have been awkward. "Actually, June thinks our mother prefers me and is proudest of me. I'd say Mom is an expert at getting what she wants and pushes June's buttons a lot. June is a wonder, she really is. And Mom is very proud of her. Of us both."

It was an intimate thing to say, to reveal that his mother was a master manipulator when it came to her children, but if Lincoln was going to be frank with his father, he'd do the same with his mother. Of course, his mother had been through a lot, but still, she was very good at manipulating her children. Lincoln and June both knew it. It wasn't a shocking thing to them anymore.

"I hoped she'd found love and settled down," Colin said after a long pause. "I wanted her to be happy."

"Oh, never doubt she's happy. She moves on when she's unhappy. I think she's in Borneo this week. She's coming to the wedding next week, but she'll only stay for the day, then trip off to wherever her new man takes her. Or her new fancy, depending on where she's at in relationships right now." Lincoln smiled, trying to puzzle out which it was with his mother now. He could never keep it straight whether she was engaged, married, or single. The status between single and engaged changed too often.

"Well, I guess happy is good," Colin said and looked over at Michael again. "Um. Could I hold him, maybe?"

"Sure," Roxie said, and Lincoln knew she'd made a decision about the man. If not, he wouldn't get anywhere near Michael. "Want me to take a picture for your family?"

"If you don't mind." Colin blushed a little and then looked over at Lincoln. "Could you sit with us?"

"Of course," Lincoln said and got up to go to the couch. He hadn't quite expected this, but he wasn't unhappy to be sitting beside the man either. There was no telling if a relationship would form from this meeting, but Lincoln had made the effort to reach out. That's all he could do.

His mother knew about the meeting and that Lincoln would be inviting Colin to the wedding. She hadn't looked pleased about it, but after a few moments of thinking, she'd nodded her head and agreed. "He is your father. I understand, Lincoln."

Lincoln had been glad to have her approval. He loved his mother, in the distant way she allowed him to, and he didn't want to make her unhappy or uncomfortable. It was good that she'd accepted his decision. It meant they could all move on.

"Can you take one with mine, too, Roxie?" Colin asked, handing his phone to her. "I don't know how that blasted thing works, but I'll figure out how to send it to my wife in a second. I just don't know how to turn the camera on."

"I'll figure it out," Roxie assured him and was soon taking pictures of Colin cradling Michael in his arms, Lincoln watching over his shoulder, with both men smiling. It was a good picture, and she had a few good ones on her phone. She'd print them out for Lincoln later and send Colin the ones she had. "The wedding will be on the beach in the back, Colin. And we can find accommodation for your family if they want to come too."

"Thank you, Roxie. I know his siblings would like to come. I'll have to talk to my wife about it. We live near Charlotte over in North Carolina now, but it's not a massive drive. I'm sure she'll want to come too." Colin fiddled with his phone before he put it down. "I've just asked her, in case we need to make arrangements."

"Great. Are you staying for dinner?" Roxie asked, taking up the question Lincoln had forgotten to ask. "I know it was a long drive for you, so you're welcome to stay the night here."

"No, I have a hotel booked. Sheryl stayed home, to let me have all the time I could with Lincoln in private. She didn't want to intrude. But I'll stay for dinner if you don't mind." Colin looked up at Lincoln, to make sure it wasn't just that Roxie was being nice. "I don't want to intrude."

"You aren't intruding, Colin. You're Lincoln's father. He asked me to make this dinner special for the occasion. It's his favorite roast," Roxie said with a patient smile. "I don't get to cook often, but I do like to when I have time. It would be great if you could stay and eat with us."

"Thanks. I appreciate that." Colin watched Roxie go as she went out of the room to put the roast on. She'd left Michael in Colin's arms. That was a very trusting thing to do. Yeah, Lincoln was right there, but if she'd been worried about the guy, she'd have taken Michael back up to Aunt Katie. "He's a handsome little fella, isn't he?"

"He is, and he's my brother," Lily said, finally coming out from behind the desk. "You can't have him."

"Oh, honey, he's not taking Michael. He's just holding him," Lincoln said as Lily flounced over to sit on Lincoln's leg.

"Are you sure?" Lily looked up at her father, her face confused. "I thought he was coming to be a daddy."

"Oh, Lily. You have to stop listening at doors. He's my father, honey. He's my dad. He came to meet me."

"Oh. Well, that's alright then. Nice to meet you." Lily stuck her hand out to Colin and Lincoln decided then and there things might just turn out alright with his father.

If Roxie and Lily approved, then he must be a

changed man. And now, he had more family than he knew what to do with, with three other half-siblings and a stepmother he hadn't met yet. It wasn't going to be lonely around here from now on. And that was just fine with Lincoln.

DARK DESIRES
~ A billionaire dark romance series ~
Dark Desire
Dark Rules
Dark Secret
Dark Time
Dark Truth

BARRE TO BAR
~ A billionaire second chance series ~
Dancing With Lies
Dancing With Temptation
Dancing With Doubt
Dancing With Guilt
Dancing With Redemption

TWISTED INTENTION
~ A billionaire revenge romance series ~
Twisted Beauty
Twisted Love
Twisted Fate

Mafia's Obsession
~ A hot mafia romance series ~
Mafia's Dirty Secret
Mafia's Fake Bride
Mafia's Final Play

Screaming Demons
~ An MC romance series full of suspense ~
Rough Start
Rough Ride
Rough Choice
Rough Patch
Rough Return
Rough Road
Rough Trip
Rough Night
Rough Love

Standalone Contemporary Romance
Billionaire in Vegas
Billionaire Hunt

Billionaire's Game

Billionaire Retreat

Billionaire On Air

A Chance To Love

Somebody To Love

Not Mine To Love

Check out Summer's entire collection at

www.summercooper.com/books